LOVEY MARY

"They met at the pump."

LOVEY MARY

BY

ALICE HEGAN RICE

AUTHOR OF

"MRS. WIGGS OF THE CABBAGE PATCH"

NEW YORK
THE CENTURY CO.
1904

THE DEVINNE PRESS.

TO

CALE YOUNG RICE

WHO TAUGHT ME THE SECRET

OF PLUCKING ROSES FROM

A CABBAGE PATCH

CONTENTS

LIST OF ILLUSTRATIONS

List of Illustrations.

xii

LOVEY MARY

LOVEY MARY

CHAPTER I

A CACTUS-PLANT

For life, with all it yields of joy and woe,
And hope and fear, . . .
Is just our chance o' the prize of learning love,—
How love might be, hath been indeed, and is.
　　　BROWNING'S "A Death in the Desert."

EVERYTHING about Lovey Mary was a contradiction, from her hands and feet, which seemed to have been meant for a big girl, to her high ideals and aspirations, that ought to have belonged to an amiable one. The only ingredient which might have reconciled all the conflicting elements in her chaotic little bosom was

3

one which no one had ever taken the trouble to supply.

When Miss Bell, the matron of the home, came to receive Lovey Mary's confession of repentance, she found her at an up-stairs window making hideous faces and kicking the furniture. The depth of her repentance could always be gaged by the violence of her conduct. Miss Bell looked at her as she would have looked at one of the hieroglyphs on the Obelisk. She had been trying to decipher her for thirteen years.

Miss Bell was stout and prim, a combination which was surely never intended by nature. Her gray dress and tight linen collar and cuffs gave the uncomfortable impression of being sewed on, while her rigid black water-waves seemed irrevocably painted upon her high forehead. She was a routinist; she believed in system, she believed in order, and she believed that godliness was akin to cleanliness. When she found an exception to a rule she regarded the exception in the light of an error. As she stood, brush in hand, before Lovey Mary, she thought for the hundredth time that the child was an exception.

"Stand up," she said firmly but not unkindly. "I thought you had too much sense to do your hair that way. Come back to the bath-room, and I will arrange it properly."

Lovey Mary gave a farewell kick at the wall before she followed Miss Bell. One side of her head was covered with tight black ringlets, and the other bristled with curl-papers.

"When I was a little girl," said Miss Bell, running the wet comb ruthlessly through the treasured curls, "the smoother my hair was the better I liked

5

it. I used to brush it down with soap and water to make it stay.''

Lovey Mary looked at the water-waves and sighed.

''If you 're ugly you never can get married with anybody, can you, Miss Bell?'' she asked in a spirit of earnest inquiry.

Miss Bell's back became stiffer, if possible, than before.

''Marriage is n't the only thing in the world. The homelier you are the better chance you have of being good. Now the Lord meant you to be plain'' —assisting Providence by drawing the braids so tight that the girl's eyebrows were elevated with the strain. ''If he had meant you to have curls he would have given them to you.''

''Well, did n't he want me to have a mother and father?'' burst forth Lovey Mary, indignantly, '' or clothes, or

6

"'Now the Lord meant you to be plain.'"

money, or nothing? Can't I ever get nothing at all 'cause I was n't started out with nothing?''

Miss Bell was too shocked to reply. She gave a final brush to the sleek, wet head and turned sorrowfully away. Lovey Mary ran after her and caught her hand.

''I 'm sorry,'' she cried impulsively. ''I want to be good. Please—please—''

Miss Bell drew her hand away coldly. ''You need n't go to Sabbath-school this morning,'' she said in an injured tone; ''you can stay here and think over what you have said. I am not angry with you. I never allow myself to get angry. I don't understand, that 's all. You are such a good girl about some things and so unreasonable about others. With a good home, good clothes, and kind treatment, what else could a girl want?''

Receiving no answer to this inquiry,

9

Miss Bell adjusted her cuffs and departed with the conviction that she had done all that was possible to throw light upon a dark subject.

Lovey Mary, left alone, shed bitter tears on her clean gingham dress. Thirteen years ought to reconcile a person even to gingham dresses with white china buttons down the back, and round straw hats bought at wholesale. But Lovey Mary's rebellion of spirit was something that time only served to increase. It had started with Kate Rider, who used to pinch her, and laugh at her, and tell the other girls to " get on to her curves." Curves had signified something dreadful to Lovey Mary; she would have experienced real relief could she have known that she did not possess any. It was not Kate Rider, however, who was causing the present tears; she had left the home two years

10

before, and her name was not allowed to be mentioned even in whispers. Neither was it rebellion against the work that had cast Lovey Mary into such depths of gloom; fourteen beds had been made, fourteen heads had been combed, and fourteen wriggling little bodies had been cheerfully buttoned into starchy blue ginghams exactly like her own.

Something deeper and more mysterious was fermenting in her soul—something that made her long passionately for the beautiful things of life, for love and sympathy and happiness; something that made her want to be good, yet tempted her constantly to rebel against her environs. It was just the world-old spirit that makes the veriest little weed struggle through a chink in the rock and reach upward toward the sun.

"What 's the matter with your hair, Lovey Mary? It looks so funny," asked a small girl, coming up the steps.

"If anybody asts you, tell 'em you don't know," snapped Lovey Mary.

"Well, Miss Bell says for you to come down to the office," said the other, unabashed. "There 's a lady down there—a lady and a baby. Me and Susie peeked in. Miss Bell made the lady cry; she made her wipe the powders off her compleshun."

"And she sent for me?" asked Lovey Mary, incredulously. Such a ripple in the still waters of the home was sufficient to interest the most disconsolate.

"Yes; and me and Susie 's going to peek some more."

Lovey Mary dried her tears and hurried down to the office. As she stood at the door she heard a girl's excited voice protesting and begging, and Miss

12

Bell's placid tones attempting to calm her. They paused as she entered.

"Mary," said Miss Bell, "you remember Kate Rider. She has brought her child for us to take care of for a while. Have you room for him in your division?"

As Lovey Mary looked at the gaily dressed girl on the sofa, her animosity rekindled. It was not Kate's bold black eyes that stirred her wrath, nor the hard red lips that recalled the taunts of other days: it was the sight of the auburn curls gathered in tantalizing profusion under the brim of the showy hat.

"Mary, answer my question!" said Miss Bell, sharply.

With an involuntary shudder of repugnance Lovey Mary drew her gaze from Kate and murmured, "Yes, 'm."

"Then you can take the baby with

13

you," continued Miss Bell, motioning to the sleeping child. "But wait a moment. I think I will put Jennie at the head of your division and let you have entire charge of this little boy. He is only a year old, Kate tells me, so will need constant attention."

Lovey Mary was about to protest, when Kate broke in:

"Oh, say, Miss Bell, please get some other girl! Tommy never would like Lovey. He's just like me: if people ain't pretty, he don't have no use for 'em."

"That will do, Kate," said Miss Bell, coldly. "It is only pity for the child that makes me take him at all. You have forfeited all claim upon our sympathy or patience. Mary, take the baby up-stairs and care for him until I come."

Lovey Mary, hot with rebellion,

14

picked him up and went out of the room. At the door she stumbled against two little girls who were listening at the keyhole.

Up-stairs in the long dormitory it was very quiet. The children had been marched away to Sunday-school, and only Lovey Mary and the sleeping baby were on the second floor. The girl sat beside the little white bed and hated the world as far as she knew it: she hated Kate for adding this last insult to the old score; she hated Miss Bell for putting this new burden on her unwilling shoulders; she hated the burden itself, lying there before her so serene and unconcerned; and most of all she hated herself.

"I wisht I was dead!" she cried passionately. "The harder I try to be good the meaner I get. Ever'body blames me, and ever'body makes fun

15

of me. Ugly old face, and ugly old hands, and straight old rat-tail hair! It ain't no wonder that nobody loves me. I just wisht I was dead!''

The sunshine came through the window and made a big white patch on the bare floor, but Lovey Mary sat in the shadow and disturbed the Sunday quiet by her heavy sobbing.

At noon, when the children returned, the noise of their arrival woke Tommy. He opened his round eyes on a strange world, and began to cry lustily. One child after another tried to pacify him, but each friendly advance increased his terror.

''Leave him be!'' cried Lovey Mary. ''Them hats is enough to skeer him into fits.'' She picked him up, and with the knack born of experience soothed and comforted him. The baby hid his face on her shoulder and held her tight. She

16

could feel the sobs that still shook the small body, and his tears were on her cheek.

"Never mind," she said. "I ain't a-going to let 'em hurt you. I 'm going to take care of you. Don't cry any more. Look!"

She stretched forth her long, unshapely hand and made grotesque snatches at the sunshine that poured in through the window. Tommy hesitated and was lost; a smile struggled to the surface, then broke through the tears.

"Look! He 's laughing!" cried Lovey Mary, gleefully. "He 's laughing 'cause I ketched a sunbeam for him!"

Then she bent impulsively and kissed the little red lips so close to her own.

17

CHAPTER II

A RUNAWAY COUPLE

"Courage mounteth with occasion."

OR two years Lovey Mary cared for Tommy: she bathed him and dressed him, taught him to walk, and kissed his bumps to make them well; she sewed for him and nursed him by day, and slept with him in her tired arms at night. And Tommy, with the inscrutable philosophy of childhood, accepted his little foster-mother and gave her his all.

One bright June afternoon the two were romping in the home yard under the beech-trees. Lovey Mary lay in the grass, while Tommy threw handfuls of

18

leaves in her face, laughing with delight at her grimaces. Presently the gate clicked, and some one came toward them.

"Good land! is that my kid?" said a woman's voice. "Come here, Tom, and kiss your mother."

Lovey Mary, sitting up, found Kate Rider, in frills and ribbons, looking with surprise at the sturdy child before her.

Tommy objected violently to this sudden overture and declined positively to acknowledge the relationship. In fact, when Kate attempted to pull him to her, he fled for protection to Lovey Mary and cast belligerent glances at the intruder.

Kate laughed.

"Oh, you need n't be so scary; you might as well get used to me, for I am going to take you home with me. I bet

2 L   19

he's a corker, ain't he, Lovey? He used to bawl all night. Sometimes I'd have to spank him two or three times.''

Lovey Mary clasped the child closer and looked up in dumb terror. Was Tommy to be taken from her? Tommy to go away with Kate?

"Great Scott!" exclaimed Kate, exasperated at the girl's manner. "You are just as ugly and foolish as you used to be. I'm going in to see Miss Bell."

Lovey Mary waited until she was in the house, then she stole noiselessly around to the office window. The curtain blew out across her cheek, and the swaying lilacs seemed to be trying to count the china buttons on her back; but she stood there with staring eyes and parted lips, and held her breath to listen.

"Of course," Miss Bell was saying, measuring her words with due preci-

"'Come here, Tom, and kiss your mother.'"

sion, "if you feel that you can now support your child and that it is your duty to take him, we cannot object. There are many other children waiting to come into the home. And yet—" Miss Bell's voice sounded human and unnatural— "yet I wish he could stay. Have you thought, Kate, of your responsibility toward him, of—"

"Oh! Ough!" shrieked Tommy from the playground, in tones of distress.

Lovey Mary left her point of vantage and rushed to the rescue. She found him emitting frenzied yells, while a tiny stream of blood trickled down his chin.

"It was my little duck," he gasped as soon as he was able to speak. "I was tissin' him, an' he bited me."

At thought of the base ingratitude on the part of the duck, Tommy wailed anew. Lovey Mary led him to the hydrant and bathed the injured lip, while

23

she soothed his feelings. Suddenly a wave of tenderness swept over her. She held his chubby face up to hers and said fervently:

"Tommy, do you love me?"

"Yes," said Tommy, with a reproachful eye on the duck. "Yes; I yuv to yuv. I don't yuv to tiss, though!"

"But me, Tommy, me. Do you love me?"

"Yes," he answered gravely, "dollar an' a half."

"Whose little boy are you?"

"Yuvey's 'e boy."

Satisfied with this catechism, she put Tommy in care of another girl and went back to her post at the window. Miss Bell was talking again.

"I will have him ready to-morrow afternoon when you come. His clothes are all in good condition. I only hope,

24

Kate, that you will care for him as tenderly as Mary has. I am afraid he will miss her sadly.''

''If he 's like me, he 'll forget about her in two or three days,'' answered the other voice. ''It always was 'out of sight, out of mind' with me.''

Miss Bell's answer was indistinct, and in a few minutes Lovey Mary heard the hall door close behind them. She shook her fists until the lilacs trembled. ''She sha'n't have him!'' she whispered fiercely. ''She sha'n't let him grow up wicked like she is. I won't let him go. I 'll hide him, I 'll—''

Suddenly she grew very still, and for a long time crouched motionless behind the bushes. The problem that faced her had but one solution, and Lovey Mary had found it.

The next morning when the sun climbed over the tree-tops and peered into the dormitory windows he found that somebody else had made an early rise. Lovey Mary was sitting by a wardrobe making her last will and testament. From the neatly folded pile of linen she selected a few garments and tied them into a bundle. Then she took out a cigar-box and gravely contemplated the contents. There were two narrow hair-ribbons which had evidently been one wide ribbon, a bit of rock crystal, four paper dolls, a soiled picture-book with some other little girl's name scratched out on the cover, and two shining silver dollars. These composed Lovey Mary's worldly possessions. She tied the money in her handkerchief and put it in her pocket, then got up softly and slipped about among the little white beds, distributing her treasures.

"I'm mad at Susie," she whispered,

pausing before a tousled head; "I hate to give her the nicest thing I 've got. But she 's just crazy 'bout picture-books."

The curious sun climbed yet a little higher and saw Lovey Mary go back to her own bed, and, rolling Tommy's clothes around her own bundle, gather the sleeping child in her arms and steal quietly out of the room. Then the sun got too high up in the heavens to watch little runaway orphan girls. Nobody saw her steal through the deserted play-room, down the clean bare steps, which she had helped to wear away, and out through the yard to the coal-shed. Here she got the reluctant Tommy into his clothes, and tied on his little round straw hat, so absurdly like her own.

"Is we playin' hie-spy, Yuvey?" asked the mystified youngster.

"Yes, Tommy," she whispered, "and

we are going a long way to hide. You are my little boy now, and you must love me better than anything in the world. Say it, Tommy; say, 'I love you better 'n anybody in the whole world.' "

"Will I det on de rollin' honor?" asked Tommy, thinking he was learning his golden text.

But Lovey Mary had forgotten her question. She was taking a farewell look at the home, every nook and corner of which had suddenly grown dear. Already she seemed a thing apart, one having no right to its shelter and protection. She turned to where Tommy was playing with some sticks in the corner, and bidding him not to stir or speak until her return, she slipped back up the walk and into the kitchen. Swiftly and quietly she made a fire in the stove and filled the kettle with water. Then she looked about for something more she might do. On the table lay the grocery book with a pencil attached. She thought a moment, then wrote laboriously under the last order: "Miss Bell I will take kere Tommy pleas dont be mad." Then she softly closed the door behind her.

A few minutes later she lifted Tommy out of the low shed window, and hurried him down the alley and out into the early morning streets. At the corner they took a car, and Tommy knelt by the window and absorbed the sights with rapt attention; to him the adventure was beginning brilliantly. Even Lovey Mary experienced a sense of exhilaration when she paid their fare out of one of the silver dollars. She knew the conductor was impressed, because he said, "You better watch Buddy's hat, ma'am." That "ma'am" pleased her profoundly; it caused her unconsciously to assume Miss Bell's tone and manner as she conversed with the back of Tommy's head.

"We 'll go out on the avenue," she said. "We 'll go from house to house till I get work. 'Most anybody would be glad to get a handy girl that can cook and wash and sew, only—I ain't very big, and then there 's you."

"Ain't that a big house?" shouted Tommy, half way out of the window.

"Yes; don't talk so loud. That 's the court-house."

"Where they make court-plaster at?" inquired Tommy shrilly.

Lovey Mary glanced around uneasily. She hoped the old man in the corner had not heard this benighted remark. All went well until the car reached the terminal station. Here Tommy refused to get off. In vain Lovey Mary coaxed and threatened.

30

"It 'll take us right back to the home," she pleaded. "Be a good boy and come with Lovey. I 'll buy you something nice."

Tommy remained obdurate. He believed in letting well enough alone. The joys of a street-car ride were present and tangible; "something nice" was vague, unsatisfying.

"Don't yer little brother want to git off?" asked the conductor, sympathetically.

"No, sir," said Lovey Mary, trying to maintain her dignity while she struggled with her charge. "If you please, sir, would you mind holding his feet while I loosen his hands?"

Tommy, shrieking indignant protests, was borne from the car and deposited on the sidewalk.

"Don't you dare get limber!" threatened Lovey Mary. "If you do I 'll spank you right here on the street. Stand up! Straighten out your legs! Tommy! do you hear me?"

Tommy might have remained limp indefinitely had not a hurdy-gurdy opportunely arrived on the scene. It is true that he would go only in the direction of the music, but Lovey Mary was delighted to have him go at all. When at last they were headed for the avenue, Tommy caused another delay.

"I want my ducky," he announced.

The words brought consternation to Lovey Mary. She had fearfully anticipated them from the moment of leaving the home.

"I 'll buy you a 'tend-like duck," she said.

"No; I want a sure-'nough ducky; I want mine."

Lovey Mary was exasperated. "Well,

32

you can't have yours. I can't get
it for you, and you might as well
hush.''

His lips trembled, and two large tears
rolled down his round cheeks. When
he was injured he was irresistible.
Lovey Mary promptly surrendered.

'' Don't cry, baby boy! Lovey 'll get
you one someway.''

For some time the quest of the duck
was fruitless. The stores they entered
were wholesale houses for the most
part, where men were rolling barrels
about or stacking skins and hides on the
sidewalk.

''Do you know what sort of a store
they sell ducks at?'' asked Lovey Mary
of a colored man who was sweeping out
an office.

''Ducks!'' repeated the negro, grin-
ning at the queerly dressed children in
their round straw hats. ''Name o' de

Lawd! What do you all want wif ducks?"

Lovey Mary explained.

"Would n't a kitten do jes as well?" he asked kindly.

"I want my ducky," whined Tommy, showing signs of returning storm.

"I don' see no way 'cept 'n' gwine to de mahket. Efen you tek de cah you kin ride plumb down dere."

Recent experience had taught Lovey Mary to be wary of street-cars, so they walked. At the market they found some ducks. The desired objects were hanging in a bunch with their limp heads tied together. Further inquiry, however, discovered some live ones in a coop.

"They 're all mama ducks," objected Tommy. "I want a baby ducky. I want my little ducky!"

When he found he could do no better,

34

he decided to take one of the large ones.
Then he said he was hungry, so he and
Mary took turn about holding it while
the other ate "po' man's pickle" and
wienerwurst.

It was two o'clock by the time they
reached the avenue, and by four they
were foot-sore and weary, but they
trudged bravely along from house to
house asking for work. As dusk came
on, the houses, which a few squares back
had been tall and imposing, seemed to
be getting smaller and more insignifi-
cant. Lovey Mary felt secure as long
as she was on the avenue. She did not
know that the avenue extended for
many miles and that she had reached
the frayed and ragged end of it. She
and Tommy passed under a bridge, and
after that the houses all seemed to be-
have queerly. Some faced one way,
some another, and crisscross between

35

them, in front of them, and behind them ran a network of railroad tracks.

"What 's the name of this street?" asked Lovey Mary of a small, barefooted girl.

"'T ain't no street," answered the little girl, gazing with undisguised amazement at the strange-looking couple; "this here is the Cabbage Patch."

"'T ain't no street . . . ; this here is the Cabbage Patch."

CHAPTER III

THE HAZY HOUSEHOLD

"Here sovereign Dirt erects her sable throne,
The house, the host, the hostess all her own."

ISS HAZY was the submerged tenth of the Cabbage Patch. The submersion was mainly one of dirt and disorder, but Miss Hazy was such a meek, inefficient little ·body that the Cabbage Patch withheld its blame and patiently tried to furnish a prop for the clinging vine. Miss Hazy, it is true, had Chris; but Chris was unstable, not only because he had lost one leg, but also because he was the wildest, noisiest, most thoughtless youngster that ever shied a rock at a lamp-post. Miss Hazy had "raised" Chris, and the neighbors had raised Miss Hazy.

When Lovey Mary stumbled over the Hazy threshold with the sleeping Tommy and the duck in her arms, Miss Hazy fluttered about in dismay. She pushed the flour-sifter farther over on the bed and made a place for Tommy, then she got a chair for the exhausted girl and hovered about her with little chirps of consternation.

"Dear sakes! You 're done tuckered out, ain't you? You an' the baby got losted? Ain't that too bad! Must I make you some tea? Only there ain't no fire in the stove. Dear me! what ever will I do? Jes wait a minute; I 'll have to go ast Mis' Wiggs."

In a few minutes Miss Hazy returned. With her was a bright-faced little woman whose smile seemed to thaw out

the frozen places in Lovey Mary's heart
and make her burst into tears on the
motherly bosom.

"There now, there," said Mrs.
Wiggs, hugging the girl up close and
patting her on the back; "there ain't
no hole so deep can't somebody pull
you out. An' here 's me an' Miss Hazy
jes waitin' to give you a h'ist."

There was something so heartsome in
her manner that Lovey Mary dried her
eyes and attempted to explain. "I 'm
tryin' to get a place," she began, "but
nobody wants to take Tommy too. I
can't carry him any further, and I don't
know where to go, and it 's 'most
night—" again the sobs choked her.

"Lawsee!" said Mrs. Wiggs, "don't
you let that worry you! I can't take
you home, 'cause Asia an' Australia
an' Europeny are sleepin' in one bed
as it is; but you kin git right in

here with Miss Hazy, can't she, Miss Hazy?''

The hostess, to whom Mrs. Wiggs was an oracle, acquiesced heartily.

''All right: that 's fixed. Now I 'll go home an' send you all over some nice, hot supper by Billy, an' to-morrow mornin' will be time enough to think things out.''

Lovey Mary, too exhausted to mind the dirt, ate her supper off a broken plate, then climbed over behind Tommy and the flour-sifter, and was soon fast asleep.

The business meeting next morning ''to think things out'' resulted satisfactorily. At first Mrs. Wiggs was inclined to ask questions and find out where the children came from, but when she saw Lovey Mary's evident distress and embarrassment, she accepted the statement that they were orphans and

that the girl was seeking work in order
to take care of herself and the boy. It
had come to be an unwritten law in the
Cabbage Patch that as few questions as
possible should be asked of strangers.
People had come there before who could
not give clear accounts of themselves.

"Now I 'll tell you what I think 'll be
best," said Mrs. Wiggs, who enjoyed
untangling snarls. "Asia kin take Mary
up to the fact'ry with her to-morrow,
an' see if she kin git her a job. I 'spect
she kin, 'cause she stands right in with
the lady boss. Miss Hazy, me an' you
kin keep a' eye on the baby between us.
If Mary gits a place she kin pay you so
much a week, an' that 'll help us all out,
'cause then we won't have to send in so
many outside victuals. If she could
make three dollars an' Chris three, you
all could git along right peart."

Lovey Mary stayed in the house most

43

of the day. She was almost afraid to look out of the little window, for fear she should see Miss Bell or Kate Rider coming. She sat in the only chair that had a bottom and diligently worked buttonholes for Miss Hazy.

"Looks like there ain't never no time to clean up," said Miss Hazy, apologetically, as she shoved Chris's Sunday clothes and a can of coal-oil behind the door.

Lovey Mary looked about her and sighed deeply. The room was brimful and spilling over: trash, tin cans, and bottles overflowed the window-sills; a crippled rocking-chair, with a faded quilt over it, stood before the stove, in the open oven of which Chris's shoe was drying; an old sewing-machine stood in the middle of the floor, with Miss Hazy's sewing on one end of it and the uncleared dinner-dishes on the other.

44

Mary could not see under the bed, but she knew from the day's experience that it was used as a combination store-room and wardrobe. She thought of the home with its bare, clean rooms and its spotless floors. She rose abruptly and went out to the rear of the house, where Tommy was playing with Europena Wiggs. They were absorbed in trying to hitch the duck to a spool-box, and paid little attention to her.

"Tommy," she said, clutching his arm, "don't you want to go back?"

But Tommy had tasted freedom; he had had one blissful day unwashed, uncombed, and uncorrected.

"No," he declared stoutly; "I 'm doin' to stay to this house and play wiv You're-a-peanut."

"Then," said Mary, with deep resignation, "the only thing for me to do is to try to clean things up."

45

When she went back into the house she untied her bundle and took out the remaining dollar.

"I 'll be back soon," she said to Miss Hazy as she stepped over a basket of potatoes. "I 'm just going over to Mrs. Wiggs's a minute."

She found her neighbor alone, getting supper. "Please, ma'am,"—she plunged into her subject at once,— "have any of your girls a dress for sale? I 've got a dollar to buy it."

Mrs. Wiggs turned the girl around and surveyed her critically. "Well, I don't know as I blame you fer wantin' to git shut of that one. There ain't more 'n room enough fer one leg in that skirt, let alone two. An' what was the sense in them big shiny buttons?"

"I don't know as it makes much difference," said Lovey Mary, disconsolately; "I 'm so ugly, nothing could make me look nice."

46

Mrs. Wiggs shook her by the shoulders good-naturedly. "Now, here," she said, "don't you go an' git sorry fer yerself! That's one thing I can't stand in nobody. There's always lots of other folks you kin be sorry fer 'stid of yerself. Ain't you proud you ain't got a harelip? Why, that one thought is enough to keep me from ever gittin' sorry fer myself."

Mary laughed, and Mrs. Wiggs clapped her hands. "That's what yer face needs—smiles! I never see anything make such a difference. But now about the dress. Yes, indeed, Asia has got dresses to give 'way. She gits 'em from Mrs. Reddin'; her husband is Mr. Bob, Billy's boss. He's a newspaper editress an' rich as cream. Mrs. Reddin' is a fallen angel, if there ever was one on this earth. She sends all sorts of clothes to Asia, an' I warm 'em over an' boil 'em down till they're her size.

47

Asia Minor!" she called to a girl who was coming in the door, "this here is Mary—Lovey Mary she calls herself, Miss Hazy's boarder. Have you got a dress you could give her?"

"I 'm going to buy it," said Mary, immediately on the defensive. She did not want them to think for a moment that she was begging. She would show them that she had money, that she was just as good as they were.

"Well, maw," the other girl was saying in a drawling voice as she looked earnestly at Lovey Mary, "seems to me she 'd look purtiest in my red dress. Her hair 's so nice an' black an' her teeth so white, I 'low the red would look best."

Mrs. Wiggs gazed at her daughter with adoring eyes. "Ain't that the artis' stickin' out through her? Could n't you tell she handles paints? Up at

48

the fact'ry she 's got a fine job, paints
flowers an' wreaths on to bath-tubs.
Yes, indeed, this here red one is what
you must have. Keep your dollar,
child; the dress never cost us a cent.
Here 's a nubia, too, you kin have; it 'll
look better than that little hat you had
on last night. That little hat worried
me; it looked like the stopper was too
little fer the bottle. There now, take
the things right home with you, an' to-
morrow you an' Asia kin start off in
style.''

Lovey Mary, flushed with the intoxication of her first compliment, went
back and tried on the dress. Miss Hazy
got so interested that she forgot to get
supper.

"You look so nice I never would 'a'
knowed you in the world!" she declared. "You don't look picked, like
you did in that other dress."

"That Wiggs girl said I looked nice in red," said Lovey Mary tentatively.

"You do, too," said Miss Hazy; "it keeps you from lookin' so corpsey. I wisht you 'd do somethin' with yer hair, though; it puts me in mind of snakes in them long black plaits."

All Lovey Mary needed was encouragement. She puffed her hair at the top and sides and tucked it up in the latest fashion. Tommy, coming in at the door, did not recognize her. She laughed delightedly.

"Do I look so different?"

"I should say you do," said Miss Hazy, admiringly, as she spread a newspaper for a table-cloth. "I never seen no one answer to primpin' like you do."

When it was quite dark Lovey Mary rolled something in a bundle and crept out of the house. After glancing cautiously up and down the tracks she made

"She puffed her hair at the
top and sides."

her way to the pond on the commons and dropped her bundle into the shallow water.

Next day, when Mrs. Schultz's goat died of convulsions, nobody knew it was due to the china buttons on Lovey Mary's gingham dress.

CHAPTER IV

AN ACCIDENT AND AN INCIDENT

"Our deeds still travel with us from afar,
And what we have been makes us what we are."

HROUGH the assistance of Asia Wiggs, Lovey Mary secured pleasant and profitable work at the factory; but her mind was not at peace. Of course it was a joy to wear the red dress and arrange her hair a different way each morning, but there was a queer, restless little feeling in her heart that spoiled even the satisfaction of looking like other girls and earning three dollars a week. The very fact that nobody took her to task, that nobody scolded or blamed her, caused her to ask herself disturbing

questions. Secret perplexity had the same effect upon her that it has upon many who are older and wiser: it made her cross.

Two days after she started to work, Asia, coming down from the decorating-room for lunch, found her in fiery dispute with a red-haired girl. There had been an accident in front of the factory, and the details were under discussion.

"Well, I know all about it," declared the red-haired girl, excitedly, "'cause my sister was the first one that got to her."

"Is your sister a nigger named Jim Brown?" asked Lovey Mary, derisively. "Ever'body says he was the first one got there."

"Was there blood on her head?" asked Asia, trying to stem the tide of argument.

"Yes, indeed," said the first speaker;

"on her head an' on her hands, too. I hanged on the steps when they was puttin' her in the ambalance-wagon, an' she never knowed a bloomin' thing!"

"Why did n't you go on with them to the hospital?" asked Lovey Mary. "I don't see how the doctors could get along without you."

"Oh, you 're just mad 'cause you did n't see her. She was awful pretty! Had on a black hat with a white feather in it, but it got in the mud. They say she had a letter in her pocket with her name on it."

"I thought maybe she come to long enough to tell you her name," teased her tormentor.

"Well, I do know it, Smarty," retorted the other, sharply: "it 's Miss Kate Rider."

Meanwhile in the Cabbage Patch Miss Hazy and Mrs. Wiggs were holding a consultation over the fence.

"She come over to my house first," Mrs. Wiggs was saying, dramatically illustrating her remarks with two tin cans. "This is me here, an' I looks up an' seen the old lady standin' over there. She put me in mind of a graven image. She had on a sorter gray mournin', did n't she, Miss Hazy?"

"Yes, 'm; that was the way it struck me. Bein' gray, I 'lowed it was fer some one she did n't keer fer pertickler."

"An' gent's cuffs," continued Mrs. Wiggs; "I noticed them right off. ''Scuse me,' says she, snappin' her mouth open an' shut like a trap—' 'scuse me, but have you seen anything of two strange children in this neighborhood?' I th'owed my apron over Lovey Mary's hat, that I was trimmin'. I was n't goin' to tell till I found out what that widder woman was after. But before I was called upon to answer, Tommy

come tearin' round the house chasin'
Cusmoodle.''

''Who?''

''Cusmoodle, the duck. I named it
this mornin'. Well, when the lady seen
Tommy she started up, then she set
down ag'in, holdin' her skirts up all
the time to keep 'em from techin' the
floor. 'How 'd they git here?' she ast,
so relieved-like that I thought she must
be kin to 'em. So I up an' told her
all I knew. I told her if she wanted
to find out anything about us she could
ast Mrs. Reddin' over at Terrace Park.
'Mrs. Robert Reddin'?' says she, lookin' dumfounded. 'Yes,' says I, 'the
finest lady, rich or poor, in Kentucky,
unless it 's her husband.' Then she
went on an' ast me goin' on a hunderd
questions 'bout all of us an' all of you
all, an' 'bout the factory. She even
ast me where we got our water at, an'

" 'She took on mighty few airs fer a
person in mournin'.' "

if you kept yer house healthy. I told her Lovey Mary had made Chris carry out more 'n a wheelbarrow full of dirt ever' night since she had been here, an' I guess it would be healthy by the time she got through.''

Miss Hazy moved uneasily. ''I told her I could n't clean up much 'count of the rheumatism, an' phthisic, an' these here dizzy spells—''

''I bet she did n't git a chance to talk much if you got started on your symptims,'' interrupted Mrs. Wiggs.

''Did n't you think she was a' awful haughty talker?''

'No, indeed. She took on mighty few airs fer a person in mournin'. When she riz to go, she says, real kind fer such a stern-faced woman, 'Do the childern seem well an' happy?' 'Yes, 'm; they 're well, all right,' says I. 'Tommy he 's like a colt what 's been

stabled up all winter an' is let out fer
the first time. As fer Mary,' I says,
'she seems kinder low in her mind, looks
awful pestered most of the time.' 'It
won't hurt her,' says the lady. 'Keep
a' eye on 'em,' says she, puttin' some
money in my hand, 'an' if you need any
more, I 'll leave it with Mrs. Reddin'.'
Then she cautioned me pertickler not to
say nothin' 'bout her havin' been here.''

"She told me not to tell, too," said
Miss Hazy; "but I don't know what
we 're goin' to say to Mrs. Schultz. She
'most sprained her back tryin' to see
who it was, an' Mrs. Eichorn come over
twicet pertendin'-like she wanted to
borrow a corkscrew driver."

"Tell 'em she was a newfangled
agent," said Mrs. Wiggs, with unblush-
ing mendacity—"a' agent fer shoe-
strings."

CHAPTER V

THE DAWN OF A ROMANCE

"There is in the worst of fortunes
The best of chances for a happy change."

OOD land! you all 're so clean in here I 'm feared of ketchin' the pneumony." Mrs. Wiggs stood in Miss Hazy's kitchen and smiled approval at the marvelous transformation.

"Well, now, I don't think it 's right healthy," complained Miss Hazy, who was sitting at the machine, with her feet on a soap-box; "so much water sloppin' round is mighty apt to give a person a cold. But Lovey Mary says she can't stand it no other way. She 's mighty set, Mis' Wiggs."

63

"Yes, an' that 's jes what you need, Miss Hazy. You never was set 'bout nothin' in yer life. Lovey Mary 's jes took you an' the house an' ever'thing in hand, an' in four weeks got you all to livin' like white folks. I ain't claimin' she ain't sharp-tongued; I 'low she 's sassed 'bout ever'body in the Patch but me by now. But she 's good, an' she 's smart, an' some of her sharp corners 'll git pecked off afore her hair grows much longer."

"Oh, mercy me! here she comes now to git her lunch," said Miss Hazy, with chagrin. "I ain't got a thing fixed."

"You go on an' sew; I 'll mess up a little somethin' fer her. She 'll stop, anyway, to talk to Tommy. Did you ever see anything to equal the way she takes on 'bout that child? She jes natchally analyzes him."

Lovey Mary, however, did not stop

as usual to play with Tommy. She came straight to the kitchen and sat down on the door-step, looking worried and preoccupied.

"How comes it you ain't singin'?" asked Mrs. Wiggs. "If I had a voice like yourn, folks would have to stop up their years with cotton. I jes find myself watchin' fer you to come home, so 's I can hear you singin' them pretty duets round the house."

Lovey Mary smiled faintly; for a month past she had been unconsciously striving to live up to Mrs. Wiggs's opinion of her, and the constant praise and commendation of that "courageous captain of compliment" had moved her to herculean effort.

But a sudden catastrophe threatened her. She sat on the door-step, white and miserable. Held tight in the hand that was thrust in her pocket was a letter; it was a blue letter addressed to Miss Hazy in large, dashing characters. Lovey Mary had got it from the postman as she went out in the morning; for five hours she had been racked with doubt concerning it. She felt that it could refer but to one subject, and that was herself. Perhaps Miss Bell had discovered her hiding-place, or, worse still, perhaps Kate Rider had seen her at the factory and was writing for Tommy. Lovey Mary crushed the letter in her hand; she would not give it to Miss Hazy. She would outwit Kate again.

"All right, honey," called Mrs. Wiggs; "here you are. 'T ain't much of a lunch, but it 'll fill up the gaps. Me an' Miss Hazy jes been talkin' 'bout you."

Lovey Mary glanced up furtively. Could they have suspected anything?

"She sat on the door-step, white
and miserable."

"Did n't yer years sorter burn? We was speakin' of the way you 'd slicked things up round here. I was a-sayin' even if you was a sorter repeatin'-rifle when it come to answerin' back, you was a good, nice girl."

Lovey Mary smoothed out the crumpled letter in her pocket. "I 'm 'fraid I ain't as good as you make me out," she said despondently.

"Oh, yes, she is," said Miss Hazy, with unusual animation; "she 's a rale good girl, when she ain't sassy."

This unexpected praise was too much for Lovey Mary. She snatched the letter from her pocket and threw it on the table, not daring to trust her good impulse to last beyond the minute.

" 'Miss Marietta Hazy, South Avenue and Railroad Crossing,' " read Mrs. Wiggs, in amazement.

"Oh, surely it ain't got me on the

69

back of it!'' cried Miss Hazy, rising hurriedly from the machine and peering over her glasses. ''You open it, Mis' Wiggs; I ain't got the nerve to.''

With chattering teeth and trembling hands Lovey Mary sat before her untasted food. She could hear Tommy's laughter through the open window, and the sound brought tears to her eyes. But Mrs. Wiggs's voice recalled her, and she nerved herself for the worst.

" *Miss Hazy.*

"DEAR MISS [Mrs. Wiggs read from the large typewritten sheet before her] : Why not study the planets and the heavens therein? In casting your future, I find that thou wilt have an active and succesful year for business, but beware of the law. You are prudent and amiable and have a lively emagination. You will have many ennemies; but fear not, for in love you will be faitful and sincer, and are fitted well fer married life."

''They surely ain't meanin' me?'' asked Miss Hazy, in great perturbation.

''*Yes, ma'am,*'' said Mrs. Wiggs, em-

70

phatically; "it 's you, plain as day. Let 's go on:

"Your star fortells you a great many lucky events. You are destined to a brilliant succes, but you will have to earn it by good conduct. Let wise men lead you. Your mildness against the wretched will bring you the friendship of everbody. Enclosed you will find a spirit picture of your future pardner. If you will send twenty-five cents with the enclosed card, which you will fill out, we will put you in direct correspondance with the gentleman, and the degree ordained by the planets will thus be fulfilled. Please show this circuler to your friends, and oblige

"Astrologer."

As the reading proceeded, Lovey Mary's fears gradually diminished, and with a sigh of relief she applied herself to her lunch. But if the letter had proved of no consequence to her, such was not the case with the two women standing at the window. Miss Hazy was re-reading the letter, vainly trying to master the contents.

"Mary," she said, "git up an' see if you can find my other pair of lookin'-

glasses. Seems like I can't git the sense
of it.''

Mrs. Wiggs meanwhile was excitedly
commenting on the charms of the
''spirit picture'':

''My, but he 's stylish! Looks fer all
the world like a' insurance agent.
Looks like he might be a little tall to his
size, but I like statute men better 'n
dumpy ones. I bet he 's got a lot of
nice manners. Ain't his smile pleasant?''

Miss Hazy seized the small picture
with trembling fingers. ''I don't seem
to git on to what it 's all about, Mis'
Wiggs. Ain't they made a mistake or
somethin'?''

''No, indeed; there 's no mistake at
all,'' declared Mrs. Wiggs. ''Yer name 's
on the back, an' it 's meant fer you.
Someway yer name 's got out as bein'
single an' needin' takin' keer of, an'

72

I reckon this here 'strologer, or conjurer, or whatever he is, seen yer good fortune in the stars an' jes wanted to let you know 'bout it.''

"Does he want to get married with her?'' asked Lovey Mary, beginning to realize the grave importance of the subject under discussion.

"Well, it may lead to that,'' answered Mrs. Wiggs, hopefully. Surely only a beneficent Providence could have offered such an unexpected solution to the problem of Miss Hazy's future.

Miss Hazy herself uttered faint protests and expostulations, but in spite of herself she was becoming influenced by Mrs. Wiggs's enthusiasm.

"Oh, shoo!'' she repeated again and again. "I ain't never had no thought of marryin'.''

"Course you ain't,'' said Mrs.

Wiggs. "Good enough reason: you ain't had a show before. Seems to me you 'd be flyin' straight in the face of Providence to refuse a stylish, sweet-smilin' man like that."

"He is fine-lookin'," acknowledged Miss Hazy, trying not to appear too pleased; "only I wisht his years did n't stick out so much."

Mrs. Wiggs was exasperated.

"Lawsee! Miss Hazy, what do you think he 'll think of yer figger? Have you got so much to brag on, that you kin go to pickin' him to pieces? Do you suppose I 'd 'a' dared to judge Mr. Wiggs that away? Why, Mr. Wiggs's nose was as long as a clothes-pin; but I would no more 'a' thought of his nose without him than I would 'a' thought of him without the nose."

"Well, what do you think I 'd orter do 'bout it?" asked Miss Hazy.

"I ain't quite made up my mind," said her mentor. "I 'll talk it over with the neighbors. But I 'spect, if we kin skeer up a quarter, that you 'll answer by the mornin's mail."

That night Lovey Mary sat in her little attic room and held Tommy close to her hungry heart. All day she worked with the thought of coming back to him at night; but with night came the dustman, and in spite of her games and stories Tommy's blue eyes would get full of the sleep-dust. To-night, however, he was awake and talkative.

"Ain't I dot no muvver?" he asked.

"No," said Lovey Mary, after a pause.

"Did n't I never had no muvver?"

Lovey Mary sat him up in her lap and looked into his round, inquiring eyes. Her very love for him hardened her heart against the one who had wronged him.

"Yes, darling, you had a mother once, but she was a bad mother, a mean, bad, wicked mother. I hate her—hate her!" Lovey Mary's voice broke in a sob.

"Ma—ry; aw, Ma—ry!" called Miss Hazy up the stairs. "You 'll have to come down here to Chris. He 's went to sleep with all his clothes on 'crost my bed, an' I can't git him up."

Lovey Mary tucked Tommy under the cover and went to Miss Hazy's assistance.

"One night I had to set up all night 'cause he would n't git up," complained Miss Hazy, in hopelessly injured tones.

Lovey Mary wasted no time in idle coaxing. She seized a broom and rapped the sleeper sharply on the legs. His peg-stick was insensible to this insult, but one leg kicked a feeble protest. In vain Lovey Mary tried violent measures; Chris simply shifted his position and slumbered on. Finally she resorted to strategy:

"Listen, Miss Hazy! Ain't that the fire-engine?"

In a moment Chris was hanging half out of the window, demanding, "Where at?"

"You great big lazy boy!" scolded Lovey Mary, as she put Miss Hazy's bed in order. "I 'll get you to behaving mighty different if I stay here long enough. What 's this?" she added, pulling something from under Miss Hazy's pillow.

"Oh, it ain't nothin'," cried Miss Hazy, reaching for it eagerly. But Lovey Mary had recognized the "spirit picture."

CHAPTER VI

THE LOSING OF MR. STUBBINS

"Love is not love
Which alters when it alteration finds,
Or bends with the remover to remove."

F the Cabbage Patch had pinned its faith upon the efficiency of the matrimonial agency in regard to the disposal of Miss Hazy, it was doomed to disappointment. The events that led up to the final catastrophe were unique in that they cast no shadows before.

Miss Hazy's letters, dictated by Mrs. Wiggs and penned by Lovey Mary, were promptly and satisfactorily answered. The original of the spirit picture proved to be one Mr. Stubbins,

" Mrs. Wiggs took pictures from her walls
and chairs from her parlor to beautify the house of Hazy."

"a prominent citizen of Bagdad Junction who desired to marry some one in the city. The lady must be of good character and without incumbrances." "That 's all right," Mrs. Wiggs had declared; "you need n't have no incumbrances. If he 'll take keer of you, we 'll all look after Chris."

The wooing had been ideally simple. Mr. Stubbins, with the impetuosity of a new lover, demanded an early meeting. It was a critical time, and the Cabbage Patch realized the necessity of making the first impression a favorable one. Mrs. Wiggs took pictures from her walls and chairs from her parlor to beautify the house of Hazy. Old Mrs. Schultz, who was confined to her bed, sent over her black silk dress for Miss Hazy to wear. Mrs. Eichorn, with deep insight into the nature of man, gave a pound-cake and a pumpkin-pie. Lovey Mary scrubbed, and dusted, and cleaned, and superintended the toilet of the bride elect.

The important day had arrived, and with it Mr. Stubbins. To the many eyes that surveyed him from behind shutters and half-open doors he was something of a disappointment. Mrs. Wiggs's rosy anticipations had invested him with the charms of an Apollo, while Mr. Stubbins, in reality, was far from godlike. "My land! he's lanker 'n a bean-pole," exclaimed Mrs. Eichorn, in disgust. But then Mrs. Eichorn weighed two hundred, and her judgment was warped. Taking everything into consideration, the prospects had been most flattering. Mr. Stubbins, sitting in Mrs. Wiggs's most comfortable chair, with a large slice of pumpkin-pie in his hand, and with Miss Hazy opposite arrayed in Mrs.

"Mr. Stubbins, sitting in Mrs. Wiggs's most comfortable chair,
with a large slice of pumpkin-pie in his hand."

Schultz's black silk, had declared himself ready to marry at once. And Mrs. Wiggs, believing that a groom in the hand is worth two in the bush, promptly precipitated the courtship into a wedding.

The affair proved the sensation of the hour, and "Miss Hazy's husband" was the cynosure of all eyes. For one brief week the honeymoon shed its beguiling light on the neighborhood, then it suffered a sudden and ignominious eclipse.

The groom got drunk.

Mary was clearing away the supper-dishes when she was startled by a cry from Miss Hazy:

"My sakes! Lovey Mary! Look at Mr. Stubbins a-comin' up the street! Do you s'pose he 's had a stroke?"

Lovey Mary ran to the window and beheld the "prominent citizen of Bagdad Junction" in a state of unmistakable intoxication. He was bareheaded and hilarious, and used the fence as a life-preserver. Miss Hazy wrung her hands and wept.

"Oh, what 'll I do?" she wailed. "I do b'lieve he 's had somethin' to drink. I ain't goin' to stay an' meet him, Mary; I 'm goin' to hide. I always was skeered of drunken men."

"I 'm not," said Mary, stoutly. "You go on up in my room and lock the door; I 'm going to stay here and keep him from messing up this kitchen. I want to tell him what I think of him, anyhow. I just hate that man! I believe you do, too, Miss Hazy."

Miss Hazy wept afresh. "Well, he ain't my kind, Mary. I know I 'd had n't orter marry him, but it 'pears like ever' woman sorter wants to try gittin' married oncet anyways. I never would 'a' done it, though, if Mrs. Wiggs had n't 'a' sicked me on."

86

By this time Mr. Stubbins had reached the yard, and Miss Hazy fled. Lovey Mary barricaded Tommy in a corner with his playthings and met the delinquent at the door. Her eyes blazed and her cheeks were aflame. This modern David had no stones and sling to slay her Góliath; she had only a vocabulary full of stinging words which she hurled forth with indignation and scorn. Mr. Stubbins had evidently been abused before, for he paid no attention to the girl's wrath. He passed jauntily to the stove and tried to pour a cup of coffee; the hot liquid missed the cup and streamed over his wrist and hand. Howling with pain and swearing vociferously, he flung the coffee-pot out of the window, kicked a chair across the room, then turned upon Tommy, who was adding shrieks of terror to the general uproar. "Stop that infernal yelling!" he cried savagely, as he struck the child full in the face with his heavy hand.

Lovey Mary sprang forward and seized the poker. All the passion of her wild little nature was roused. She stole up behind him as he knelt before Tommy, and lifted the poker to strike. A pair of terrified blue eyes arrested her. Tommy forgot to cry, in sheer amazement at what she was about to do. Ashamed of herself, she threw the poker aside, and taking advantage of Mr. Stubbins's crouching position, she thrust him suddenly backward into the closet. The manœuver was a brilliant one, for while Mr. Stubbins was unsteadily separating himself from the debris into which he had been cast, Lovey Mary slammed the door and locked it. Then she picked up Tommy and fled out of the house and across the yard.

Mrs. Wiggs was sitting on her back porch pretending to knit, but in truth absorbed in a wild game of tag which the children were having on the commons. "That 's right," she was calling excitedly—"that 's right, Chris Hazy! You kin ketch as good as any of 'em, even if you have got a peg-stick." But when she caught sight of Mary's white, distressed face and Tommy's streaming eyes, she dropped her work and held out her arms. When Mary had finished her story Mrs. Wiggs burst forth:

"An' to think I run her up ag'in' this! Ain't men deceivin'? Now I 'd 'a' risked Mr. Stubbins myself fer the askin'. It 's true he was a widower, an' ma uster allays say, 'Don't fool with widowers, grass nor sod.' But Mr. Stubbins was so slick-tongued! He told me yesterday he had to take liquor sometime fer his war enjury."

"But, Mrs. Wiggs, what must we do?" asked Lovey Mary, too absorbed in the present to be interested in the past.

"Do? Why, we got to git Miss Hazy out of this here hole. It ain't no use consultin' her; I allays have said talkin' to Miss Hazy was like pullin' out bastin'-threads: you jes take out what you put in. Me an' you has got to think out a plan right here an' now, then go to work an' carry it out."

"Could n't we get the agency to take him back?" suggested Mary.

"No, indeed; they could n't afford to do that. Lemme see, lemme see—" For five minutes Mrs. Wiggs rocked meditatively, soothing Tommy to sleep as she rocked. When she again spoke it was with inspiration:

"I 've got it! It looks sometime, Lovey Mary, 's if I 'd sorter caught

some of Mr. Wiggs's brains in thinkin'
things out. They ain't but one thing to
do with Miss Hazy's husband, an' we 'll
do it this very night.''

"What, Mrs. Wiggs? What is it?"
asked Lovey Mary, eagerly.

"Why, to lose him, of course! We 'll
wait till Mr. Stubbins is dead asleep;
you know men allays have to sleep off
a jag like this. I 've seen Mr. Wiggs—
I mean I 've heared 'em say so many
a time. Well, when Mr. Stubbins is
sound asleep, you an' me an' Billy will
drag him out to the railroad.''

Mrs. Wiggs's voice had sunk to a
hoarse whisper, and her eyes looked
fierce in the twilight.

Lovey Mary shuddered.

"You ain't going to let the train run
over him, are you?" she asked.

"Lor', child, I ain't a 'sassinator!
No; we 'll wait till the midnight freight

91

comes along, an' when it stops fer water, we 'll h'ist Mr. Stubbins into one of them empty cars. The train goes 'way out West somewheres, an' by the time Mr. Stubbins wakes up, he 'll be so far away from home he won't have no money to git back.''

''What 'll Miss Hazy say?'' asked Mary, giggling in nervous excitement.

''Miss Hazy ain't got a thing to do with it,'' replied Mrs. Wiggs conclusively.

At midnight, by the dark of the moon, the unconscious groom was borne out of the Hazy cottage. Mrs. Wiggs carried his head, while Billy Wiggs and Mary and Asia and Chris officiated at his arms and legs. The bride surveyed the scene from the chinks of the upstairs shutters.

Silently the little group waited until the lumbering freight train slowed up to take water, then with a concerted effort they lifted the heavy burden into an empty car. As they shrank back into the shadow, Billy whispered to Lovey Mary:

"Say, what was that you put 'longside of him?"

Mary looked shamefaced.

"It was just a little lunch-dinner," she said apologetically; "it seemed sorter mean to send him off without anything to eat."

"Gee!" said Billy. "You 're a cur'us girl!"

The engine whistled, and the train moved thunderously away, bearing an unconscious passenger, who, as far as the Cabbage Patch was concerned, was henceforth submerged in the darkness of oblivion.

CHAPTER VII

NEIGHBORLY ADVICE

"It's a poor business looking at the sun with a cloudy face."

THE long, hot summer days that followed were full of trials for Lovey Mary. Day after day the great unwinking sun glared savagely down upon the Cabbage Patch, upon the stagnant pond, upon the gleaming rails, upon the puffing trains that pounded by hour after hour. Each morning found Lovey Mary trudging away to the factory, where she stood all day counting and sorting and packing tiles. At night she climbed wearily to her little room under the roof, and tried to sleep with a wet

94

cloth over her face to keep her from smelling the stifling car smoke.

But it was not the heat and discomfort alone that made her cheeks thin and her eyes sad and listless: it was the burden on her conscience, which seemed to be growing heavier all the time. One morning Mrs. Wiggs took her to task for her gloomy countenance. They met at the pump, and, while the former's bucket was being filled, Lovey Mary leaned against a lamp-post and waited in a dejected attitude.

"What 's the matter with you?" asked Mrs. Wiggs. " What you lookin' so wilted about?"

Lovey Mary dug her shoe into the ground and said nothing. Many a time had she been tempted to pour forth her story to this friendly mentor, but the fear of discovery and her hatred of Kate deterred her.

Mrs. Wiggs eyed her keenly. "Pesterin' about somethin'?" she asked.

"Yes, 'm," said Lovey Mary, in a low tone.

"Somethin' that 's already did?"

"Yes, 'm"—still lower.

"Did you think you was actin' fer the best?"

The girl lifted a pair of honest gray eyes. "Yes, ma'am, I did."

"I bet you did!" said Mrs. Wiggs, heartily. "You ain't got a deceivin' bone in yer body. Now what you want to do is to brace up yer sperrits. The decidin'-time was the time fer worryin'. You 've did what you thought was best; now you want to stop thinkin' 'bout it. You don't want to go round turnin' folks' thoughts sour jes to look at you. Most girls that had white teeth like you would be smilin' to show 'em, if fer nothin' else."

96

"I wisht I was like you," said Lovey Mary.

"Don't take it out in wishin'. If you want to be cheerful, jes set yer mind on it an' do it. Can't none of us help what traits we start out in life with, but we kin help what we end up with. When things first got to goin' wrong with me, I says: 'O Lord, whatever comes, keep me from gittin' sour!' It was n't fer my own sake I ast it,—some people 'pears to enjoy bein' low-sperrited,— it was fer the childern an' Mr. Wiggs. Since then I 've made it a practice to put all my worries down in the bottom of my heart, then set on the lid an' smile."

"But you think ever'body 's nice and good," complained Lovey Mary. "You never see all the meanness I do."

"Don't I? I been watchin' old man Rothchild fer goin' on eleven year', tryin' to see some good in him, an' I never found it till the other day when I seen him puttin' a splint on Cusmoodle's broken leg. He's the savagest man I know, yit he keered fer that duck as tender as a woman. But it ain't jes seein' the good in folks an' sayin' nice things when you're feelin' good. The way to git cheerful is to smile when you feel bad, to think about somebody else's headache when yer own is 'most bustin', to keep on believin' the sun is a-shinin' when the clouds is thick enough to cut. Nothin' helps you to it like thinkin' more 'bout other folks than about yerself."

"I think 'bout Tommy first," said Lovey Mary.

"Yes, you certainly do yer part by him. If my childern wore stockin's an' got as many holes in 'em as he does, I'd work buttonholes in 'em at the start

98

fer the toes to come through. But even Tommy wants somethin' besides darns. Why don't you let him go barefoot on Sundays, too, an' take the time you been mendin' fer him to play with him? I want to see them pretty smiles come back in yer face ag'in.''

In a subsequent conversation with Miss Hazy, Mrs. Wiggs took a more serious view of Lovey Mary's depression·

''She jes makes.me wanter cry, she's so subdued-like. I never see anybody change so in my life. It 'u'd jes be a relief to hear her sass some of us like she uster. She told me she never had nobody make over her like we all did, an' it sorter made her 'shamed. Lawsee! if kindness is goin' to kill her, I think we'd better fuss at her some.''

'''Pears to me like she's got nervous sensations,'' said Miss Hazy; ''she jumps up in her sleep, an' talks 'bout folks an' things I never heared tell of.''

"That 's exactly what ails her," agreed Mrs. Wiggs: "it 's nerves, Miss Hazy. To my way of thinkin', nerves is worser than tumors an' cancers. Look at old Mrs. Schultz. She 's got the dropsy so bad you can't tell whether she 's settin' down or standin' up, yet she ain't got a nerve in her body, an' has 'most as good a time as other folks. We can't let Lovey Mary go on with these here nerves; no tellin' where they 'll land her at. If it was jes springtime, I 'd give her sulphur an' molasses an' jes a leetle cream of tartar; that, used along with egg-shell tea, is the outbeatenest tonic I ever seen. But I never would run ag'in' the seasons. Seems to me I 've heared yallerroot spoke of fer killin' nerves.''

"I don't 'spect we could git no yaller-root round here.''

"What 's the matter with Miss Viny? I bet it grows in her garden thick as hairs on a dog's back. Let 's send Lovey Mary out there to git some, an' we 'll jes repeat the dose on her till it takes some hold."

"I ain't puttin' much stock in Miss Viny," demurred Miss Hazy. "I 've heared she was a novelist reader, an' she ain't even a church-member."

"An' do you set up to jedge her?" asked Mrs. Wiggs, in fine scorn. "Miss Viny 's got more sense in her little finger than me an' you has got in our whole heads. She can doctor better with them yarbs of hers than any physicianner I know. As to her not bein' a member, she lives right an' helps other folks, an' that 's more than lots of members does. Besides," she added conclusively, "Mr. Wiggs himself was n't no church-member."

CHAPTER VIII

A DENOMINATIONAL GARDEN

"Oh, mickle is the powerful grace that lies
  In herbs, plants, stones, and their true qualities;
For naught so vile that on the earth doth live
But to the earth some special good doth give."

THE following Sunday being decidedly cooler, Lovey Mary was started off to Miss Viny's in quest of yellowroot. She had protested that she was not sick, but Miss Hazy, backed by Mrs. Wiggs, had insisted.

"If you git down sick, it would be a' orful drain on me," was Miss Hazy's final argument, and the point was effective.

As Lovey Mary trudged along the railroad-tracks, she was unconscious of the pleasant changes of scenery. The

102

cottages became less frequent, and the bare, dusty commons gave place to green fields. Here and there a tree spread its branches to the breezes, and now and then a snatch of bird song broke the stillness. But Lovey Mary kept gloomily on her way, her eyes fixed on the cross-ties. The thoughts surging through her brain were dark enough to obscure even the sunshine. For three nights she had cried herself to sleep, and the "nervous sensations" were getting worse instead of better.

"Just two months since Kate was hurt," she said to herself. "Soon as she gets out the hospital she 'll be trying to find us again. I believe she was coming to the factory looking for me when she got run over. She 'd just like to take Tommy away and send me to jail. Oh, I hate her worse all the time! I wish she was—"

103

The wish died on her lips, for she suddenly realized that it might already have been fulfilled. Some one coughed near by, and she started guiltily.

"You seem to be in a right deep steddy," said a voice on the other side of the fence.

Lovey Mary glanced up and saw a queer-looking old woman smiling at her quizzically. A pair of keen eyes twinkled under bushy brows, and a fierce little beard bristled from her chin. When she smiled it made Lovey Mary think of a pebble dropped in a pool, for the wrinkles went rippling off from her mouth in ever-widening circles until they were lost in the gray hair under her broad-brimmed hat.

"Are you Miss Viny?" asked Lovey Mary, glancing at the old-fashioned flower-garden beyond.

"Well, I been that fer sixty year';

104

I ain't heared of no change," answered the old lady.

"Miss Hazy sent me after some yellowroot," said Lovey Mary, listlessly.

"Who fer?"

"Me."

Miss Viny took a pair of large spectacles from her pocket, put them on the tip of her nose, and looked over them critically at Lovey Mary.

"Stick out yer tongue."

Lovey Mary obeyed.

"Uh-huh. It 's a good thing I looked. You don't no more need yallerroot than a bumblebee. You come in here on the porch an' tell me what 's ailin' you, an' I 'll do my own prescriptin'."

Lovey Mary followed her up the narrow path, that ran between a mass of flowers. Snowy oleanders, yellow asters, and purple phlox crowded together in

105

a space no larger than Miss Hazy's front yard. Lovey Mary forgot her troubles in sheer delight in seeing so many flowers together.

"Do you love 'em, too?" asked Miss Viny, jerking her thumb over her shoulder.

"I guess I would if I had a chance. I never saw them growing out of doors like this. I always had to look at them through the store windows."

"Oh, law, don't talk to me 'bout caged-up flowers! I don't b'lieve in shuttin' a flower up in a greenhouse any more 'n I b'lieve in shuttin' myself up in one church."

Lovey Mary remembered what Miss Hazy had told her of Miss Viny's pernicious religious views, and she tried to change the subject. But Miss Viny was started upon a favorite theme and was not to be diverted.

"'Stick out yer tongue.'"

"This here is a denominational garden, an' I got every congregation I ever heared of planted in it. I ain't got no faverite bed. I keer fer 'em all jes alike. When you come to think of it, the same rule holds good in startin' a garden as does in startin' a church. You first got to steddy what sort of soil you goin' to work with, then you have to sum up all the things you have to fight ag'inst. Next you choose what flowers are goin' to hold the best places. That 's a mighty important question in churches, too, ain't it? Then you go to plantin', the thicker the better, fer in both you got to allow fer a mighty fallin' off. After that you must take good keer of what you got, an' be sure to plant something new each year. Once in a while some of the old growths has to be thinned out, and the new upstarts an' suckers has to be pulled up. Now, if you 'll come out here I 'll show you round.''

She started down the path, and Lovey Mary, somewhat overwhelmed by this oration, followed obediently.

''These here are the Baptists,'' said Miss Viny, waving her hand toward a bed of heliotrope and flags. ''They want lots of water; like to be wet clean through. They sorter set off to they-selves an' tend to their own business; don't keer much 'bout minglin' with the other flowers.''

Lovey Mary did not understand very clearly what Miss Viny was talking about, but she was glad to follow her in the winding paths, where new beauties were waiting at every turn.

''These is geraniums, ain't they? One of the girls had one, once, in a flower-pot when she was sick.''

''Yes,'' said Miss Viny; ''they 're
110

Methodist. They fall from grace an' has to be revived; they like lots of encouragement in the way of sun an' water. These phlox are Methodist, too; no set color, easy to grow, hardy an' vigorous. Pinchin' an' cuttin' back the shoots makes it flower all the better; needs new soil every few years; now ain't that Methodist down to the ground?"

"Are there any Presbyterians?" asked Lovey Mary, beginning to grasp Miss Viny's meaning.

"Yes, indeed; they are a good, old, reliable bed. Look at all these roses an' tiger-lilies an' dahlias; they all knew what they was goin' to be afore they started to grow. They was elected to it, an' they 'll keep on bein' what they started out to be clean to the very end."

"I know about predestination," cried

Lovey Mary, eagerly. "Miss Bell used to tell us all those things."

"Who did?"

Lovey Mary flushed crimson. "A lady I used to know," she said evasively.

Miss Viny crossed the garden, and stopped before a bed of stately lilies and azaleas. "These are 'Piscopals," she explained. "Ain't they tony? Jes look like they thought their bed was the only one in the garden. Somebody said that a lily did n't have no pore kin among the flowers. It ain't no wonder they 'most die of dignity. They 're like the 'Piscopals in more ways 'n one; both hates to be disturbed, both likes some shade, an' "— confidentially — "both air pretty pernickity. But to tell you the truth, ain't nothin' kin touch 'em when it comes to beauty! I think all the other beds is proud of 'em, if

112

you 'd come to look into it. Why, look at weddin's an' funerals! Don't all the churches call in the 'Piscopals an' the lilies on both them occasions?''

Lovey Mary nodded vaguely.

"An' here," continued Miss Viny, "are the Unitarians. You may be s'prised at me fer havin' 'em in here, 'long with the orthodox churches; but if the sun an' the rain don't make no distinction, I don't see what right I got to put 'em on the other side of the fence. These first is sweet-william, as rich in bloom as the Unitarian is in good works, a-sowin' theyselves constant, an' every little plant a-puttin' out a flower.''

"Ain't there any Catholics?" asked Lovey Mary.

"Don't you see them hollyhawks an' snowballs an' laylacs? All of them are Catholics, takin' up lots of room an'

113

needin' the prunin'-knife pretty often,
but bringin' cheer and brightness to the
whole garden when it needs it most.
Yes, I guess you'd have trouble thinkin'
of any sect I ain't got planted. Them
ferns over in the corner is Quakers. I
ain't never seen no Quakers, but they
tell me that they don't b'lieve in flow-
erin' out; that they like coolness an'
shade an' quiet, an' are jes the same the
year round. These colea plants are the
apes; they are all things to all men,
take on any color that 's round 'em, kin
be the worst kind of Baptists or Presbyterians, but if left to theyselves they
run back to good-fer-nothin's. This
here everlastin' is one of these here
Christians that 's so busy thinkin' 'bout
dyin' that he fergits to live.''

Miss Viny chuckled as she crumbled
the dry flower in her fingers.

''See how different this is,'' she said,

plucking a sprig of lemon-verbena. " This an' the mint an' the sage an' the lavender is all true Christians; jes by bein' touched they give out a' influence that makes the whole world a sweeter place to live in. But, after all, they can't all be alike! There 's all sorts of Christians: some stands fer sunshine, some fer shade; some fer beauty, some fer use; some up high, some down low. There 's jes one thing all the flowers has to unite in fightin' ag'inst—that 's the canker-worm, Hate. If it once gits in a plant, no matter how good an' strong that plant may be, it eats right down to its heart."

"How do you get it out, Miss Viny?" asked Lovey Mary, earnestly.

"Prayer an' perseverance. If the Christian 'll do his part, God 'll do his 'n. You see, I 'm tryin' to be to these flowers what God is to his

churches. The sun, which answers to
the Sperrit, has to shine on 'em all, an'
the rain, which answers to God's mercy,
has to fall on 'em all. I jes watch 'em,
an' plan fer 'em, an' shelter 'em, an'
love 'em, an' if they do their part
they 're bound to grow. Now I 'm
goin' to cut you a nice bo'quet to carry
back to the Cabbage Patch.''

So engrossed were the two in select-
ing and arranging the flowers that
neither thought of the yellowroot or
its substitute. Nevertheless, as Lovey
Mary tramped briskly back over the
railroad-ties with her burden of blos-
soms, she bore a new thought in her
heart which was destined to bring about
a surer cure than any of Miss Viny's
most efficient herbs

CHAPTER IX

"And cloudy the day, or stormy the night,
The sky of her heart was always bright."

"IT would n't s'prise me none if we had cyclones an' tornadoes by evenin', it looks so thundery outdoors."

It was inconsiderate of Miss Hazy to make the above observation in the very face of the most elaborate preparations for a picnic, but Miss Hazy's evil predictions were too frequent to be effective.

"I 'll scurry round an' git another loaf of bread," said Mrs. Wiggs, briskly, as she put a tin pail into the corner of the basket. "Lovey Mary,

117

you put in the eggs an' git them cookies outen the stove. I promised them boys a picnic on Labor Day, an' we are goin' if it snows."

"Awful dangerous in the woods when it storms," continued Miss Hazy. "I heared of a man oncet that would go to a picnic in the rain, and he got struck so bad it burned his shoes plump off."

"Must have been the same man that got drownded, when he was little, fer goin' in swimmin' on Sunday," answered Mrs. Wiggs, wiping her hands on her apron.

"Mebbe 't was," said Miss Hazy.

Lovey Mary vibrated between the door and the window, alternating between hope and despair. She had set her heart on the picnic with the same intensity of desire that had characterized her yearning for goodness and affection and curly hair.

118

"I believe there is a tiny speck more blue," she said, scanning the heavens for the hundredth time.

"Course there is!" cried Mrs. Wiggs, "an' even if there ain't, we 'll have the picnic anyway. I b'lieve in havin' a good time when you start out to have it. If you git knocked out of one plan, you want to git yerself another right quick, before yer sperrits has a chance to fall. Here comes Jake an' Chris with their baskets. Suppose you rench off yer hands an' go gether up the rest of the childern. I 'spect Billy 's done hitched up by this time."

At the last moment Miss Hazy was still trying to make up her mind whether or not she would go. " Them wheels don't look none too stiddy fer sich a big load," she said cautiously.

"Them wheels is a heap sight stiddier than your legs," declared Mrs. Wiggs.

119

"An' there ain't a meeker hoss in Kentucky than Cuby. He looks like he might 'a' belonged to a preacher 'stid of bein' a broken-down engine-hoss."

An unforeseen delay was occasioned by a heated controversy between Lovey Mary and Tommy concerning the advisability of taking Cusmoodle.

"There ain't more than room enough to squeeze you in, Tommy," she said, "let alone that fat old duck."

" 'T ain't a fat old duck."

" 'T is, too! He sha'n't go. You 'll have to stay at home yourself if you can't be good."

"I feel like I was doin' to det limber," threatened Tommy.

Mrs. Wiggs recognized a real danger. She also knew that discretion was the better part of valor. "Here 's a nice little place up here by me, jes big enough fer you an' Cusmoodle. You

kin set on the basket; it won't mash
nothin'. If we 're packed in good an'
tight, can't none of us fall out.''

When the last basket was stored
away, the party started off in glee,
leaving Miss Hazy still irresolute in
the doorway, declaring that ''she almost wisht she had 'a' went.''

The destination had not been decided
upon, so it was discussed as the wagon
jolted along over the cobblestones.

''Let 's go out past Miss Viny's,''
suggested Jake; ''there 's a bully woods
out there.''

''Aw, no! Let 's go to Tick Creek
an' go in wadin'.''

Mrs. Wiggs, seated high above the
party and slapping the reins on Cuba's
back, allowed the lively debate to con-
tinue until trouble threatened, then she
interfered:

''I think it would be nice to go over

121

to the cemetery. We 'd have to cross the city, but when you git out there there 's plenty of grass an' trees, an' it runs right 'longside the river.''

The proximity of the river decided the matter.

''I won't hardly take a swim!'' said Jake, going through the motions, to the discomfort of the two little girls who were hanging their feet from the back of the wagon.

''I 'm afraid it 's going to rain so hard that you can take your swim before you get there,'' said Lovey Mary, as the big drops began to fall.

The picnic party huddled on the floor of the wagon in a state of great merriment, while Mrs. Wiggs spread an old quilt over as many of them as it would cover.

'' 'T ain't nothin' but a summer shower,'' she said, holding her head on

one side to keep the rain from driving
in her face. "I 'spect the sun is shinin'
at the cemetery right now."

As the rickety wagon, with its
drenched and shivering load, rattled
across Main street, an ominous sound
fell upon the air:

One—two—three! One—two!

Mrs. Wiggs wrapped the lines about
her wrists and braced herself for the
struggle. But Cuba had heard the summons, his heart had responded to the
old call, and with one joyous bound
he started for the fire.

"Hold on tight!" yelled Mrs. Wiggs.
"Don't none of you fall out. Whoa,
Cuby! Whoa! I 'll stop him in a
minute. Hold tight!"

Cuba kicked the stiffness out of his
legs, and laying his ears back, raced
valiantly for five squares neck and neck
with the engine-horses. But the odds

were against him; Mrs. Wiggs and Chris sawing on one line, and Billy and Jake pulling on the other, proved too heavy a handicap. Within sight of the fire he came to a sudden halt.

"It 's the lumber-yards!" called Chris, climbing over the wheels. "Looks like the whole town 's on fire."

"Let 's unhitch Cuby an' tie him, an' stand in the wagon an' watch it," cried Mrs. Wiggs, in great excitement.

The boys were not content to be stationary, so they rushed away, leaving Mrs. Wiggs and the girls, with Tommy and the duck, to view the conflagration at a safe distance.

For two hours the fire raged, leaping from one stack of lumber to another, and threatening the adjacent buildings. Every fire-engine in the department was called out, the commons were black with people, and the excitement was intense.

124

"Ain't you glad we come?" cried Lovey Mary, dancing up and down in the wagon.

"We never come. We was brought," said Asia.

Long before the fire was under control the sun had come through the clouds and was shining brightly. Picnics, however, were not to be considered when an attraction like this was to be had. When the boys finally came straggling back the fire was nearly out, the crowd had dispersed, and only the picnic party was left on the commons.

"It 's too late to start to the cemetery," said Mrs. Wiggs, thoughtfully. "What do you all think of havin' the picnic right here an' now?"

The suggestion was regarded as nothing short of an inspiration.

"The only trouble," continued Mrs. Wiggs, "is 'bout the water. Where we

125

goin' to git any to drink? I know one of the firemen, Pete Jenkins; if I could see him I 'd ast him to pour us some outen the hose.''

''Gimme the pail; I 'll go after him,'' cried Jake.

''Naw, you don't; I 'm a-goin'. It 's my maw that knows him,'' said Billy.

''That ain't nothin'. My uncle knows the chief of police! Can't I go, Mrs. Wiggs?''

Meanwhile Chris had seized the hint and the bucket, and was off in search of Mr. Peter Jenkins, whose name would prove an open sesame to that small boy's paradise—the engine side of the rope.

The old quilt, still damp, was spread on the ground, and around it sat the picnic party, partaking ravenously of dry sandwiches and cheese and cheer. Such laughing and crowding and romp-

ing as there was! Jake gave correct
imitations of everybody in the Cabbage
Patch, Chris did some marvelous stunts
with his wooden leg, and Lovey Mary
sang every funny song that she knew.
Mrs. Wiggs stood in the wagon above
them, and dispensed hospitality as long
as it lasted. Cuba, hitched to a fence
near by, needed no material nourish-
ment. He was contentedly sniffing the
smoke-filled air, and living over again
the days of his youth.

When the party reached home, tired
and grimy, they were still enthusiastic
over the fine time they had had.

"It 's jes the way I said," proclaimed
Mrs. Wiggs, as she drove up with a
flourish; "you never kin tell which way
pleasure is a-comin'. Who ever would
'a' thought, when we aimed at the cemetery, that we 'd land up at a first-class
fire?"

CHAPTER X

A TIMELY VISIT

"The love of praise, howe'er concealed by art,
Reigns more or less, and glows in ev'ry heart."

EEKS and months slip-
ped by, and the Cab-
bage Patch ate break-
fast and supper by
lamplight. Those who
could afford it were
laying in their winter coal, and those
who could not were providently pasting
brown paper over broken window-panes,
and preparing to keep Jack Frost at bay
as long as possible.

One Saturday, as Lovey Mary came
home from the factory, she saw a well-
dressed figure disappearing in the
distance.

128

"Who is that lady?" she demanded suspiciously of Europena Wiggs, who was swinging violently on the gate.

"'T ain't no lady," said Europena. "It 's my Sunday-school teacher."

"Mrs. Redding?"

"Uh-huh. She wants Asia to come over to her house this evenin'."

"Wisht I could go," said Lovey Mary.

"Why can't you?" asked Mrs. Wiggs, coming to the open door. "Asia would jes love to show Mrs. Reddin' how stylish you look in that red dress. I 'll curl yer hair on the poker if you want me to."

Any diversion from the routine of work was acceptable, so late that afternoon the two girls, arrayed in their best garments, started forth to call on the Reddings.

"I wisht I had some gloves," said

129

Lovey Mary, rubbing her blue fingers.

"If I 'd 'a' thought about it I 'd 'a' made you some before we started. It don't take no time." Asia held out her hands, which were covered with warm red mitts. "I make 'em outen Billy's old socks after the feet 's wore off."

"I don't see how you know how to do so many things!" said Lovey Mary, admiringly.

"'T ain't nothin'," disclaimed Asia, modestly. "It 's jes the way maw brought us up. Whenever we started out to do a thing she made us finish it someway or 'nother. Oncet when we was all little we lived in the country. She sent Billy out on the hoss to git two watermelon, an' told him fer him not to come home without 'em. When Billy got out to the field he found all the watermelon so big he could n't carry

130

"Asia held out her hands, which
were covered with warm
red mitts."

one, let alone two. What do you think he done?"

"Come home without 'em?"

"No, sir, he never! He jes set on the fence an' thought awhile, then he took offen his jeans pants an' put a watermelon in each leg an' hanged 'em 'crost old Rollie's back an' come ridin' home barelegged."

"I think he 's the nicest boy in the Cabbage Patch," said Lovey Mary, laughing over the incident. "He never does tease Tommy."

"That 's 'cause he likes you. He says you 've got grit. He likes the way you cleaned up Miss Hazy an' stood up to Mr. Stubbins."

A deeper color than even the fresh air warranted came into Lovey Mary's cheeks, and she walked on for a few minutes in pleased silence.

"Don't you want to wear my gloves awhile?" asked Asia.

"No; my hands ain't cold any more," said Lovey Mary.

As they turned into Terrace Park, with its beautiful grounds, its fountains and statuary, Asia stopped to explain.

"Jes rich folks live over here. That there is the Reddin's' house, the big white one where them curbstone ladies are in the yard. I wisht you could git a peek in the parlor; they 've got chairs made outer real gold, an' strandaliers that look like icicles all hitched together."

"Do they set on the gold chairs?"

"No, indeed; the legs is too wabbly fer that. I reckon they 're jes to show how rich they are. This here is where the carriage drives in. Their hired man wears a high-style hat, an' a fur cape jes like Mrs. Reddin's."

"I 'spect they have turkey every day, don't they, Asia?"

Before Asia's veracity was tested to the limit, the girls were startled by the sudden appearance of an excited housemaid at the side door.

"Simmons! Simmons!" she screamed. "Oh, where is that man? I 'll have to go for somebody myself." And without noticing the girls, she ran hastily down the driveway.

Asia, whose calmness was seldom ruffled, led the way into the entry. "That 's the butter's pantry," she said, jerking her thumb over her shoulder.

"Don't they keep nothing in it but butter?" gasped Lovey Mary.

"Reckon not. They 've got a great big box jes fer ice; not another thing goes in it."

Another maid ran down the steps, calling Simmons.

135

Asia, a frequent visitor at the house, made her way unconcernedly up to the nursery. On the second floor there was great confusion; the telephone was ringing, servants were hurrying to and fro.

"He 'll choke to death before the doctor gets here!" they heard the nurse say as she ran through the hall. From the open nursery door they could hear the painful gasps and coughs of a child in great distress.

Asia paused on the landing, but Lovey Mary darted forward. The mother instinct, ever strong within her, had responded instantly to the need of the child. In the long, dainty room full of beautiful things, she only saw the terrified baby on his mother's lap, his face purple, his eyes distended, as he fought for his breath.

Without a word she sprang forward,

"Master Robert Redding was right side up again,
sobbing himself quiet in Lovey Mary's arms."

and grasping the child by his feet, held him at arm's-length and shook him violently. Mrs. Redding screamed, and the nurse, who was rushing in with hot milk, dropped the cup in horror. But a tiny piece of hard candy lay on the floor, and Master Robert Redding was right side up again, sobbing himself quiet in Lovey Mary's arms.

After the excitement had subsided, and two doctors and Mr. Redding had arrived breathless upon the scene, Mrs. Redding, for the dozenth time, lavished her gratitude upon Lovey Mary:

"And to think you saved my precious baby! The doctor said it was the only thing that could have saved him, yet we four helpless women had no idea what to do. How did you know, dear? Where did you ever see it done?"

Lovey Mary, greatly abashed, faced the radiant parents, the two portly doctors, and the servants in the background.

"I learned on Tommy," she said in a low voice. "He swallered a penny once that we was going to buy candy with. I did n't have another, so I had to shake it out."

During the laugh that followed, she and Asia escaped, but not before Mr. Redding had slipped a bill into her hand, and the beautiful Mrs. Redding had actually given her a kiss!

CHAPTER XI

THE CHRISTMAS PLAY

"Not failure, but low aim, is crime."

S the holiday season approached, a rumor began to be circulated that the Cabbage Patch Sunday-school would have an entertainment as well as a Christmas tree. The instigator of this new movement was Jake Schultz, whose histrionic ambition had been fired during his apprenticeship as "super" at the opera-house.

"I know a man what rents costumes, an' the promp'-books to go with 'em," he said to several of the boys one Sunday afternoon. "If we all chip in we

kin raise the price, an' git it back easy
by chargin' admittance.''

''Aw, shucks!'' said Chris. ''We
don't know nothin' 'bout play-actin'.''

''We kin learn all right,'' said Billy
Wiggs. ''I bid to be the feller that acts
on the trapeze.''

The other boys approving of the plan,
it was agreed that Jake should call on
the costumer at his earliest convenience.

One night a week later Lovey Mary
was getting supper when she heard an
imperative rap on the door. It was
Jake Schultz. He mysteriously beckoned her out on the steps, and closed
the door behind them.

''Have you ever acted any?'' he
asked.

''I used to say pieces at the home,''
said Lovey Mary, forgetting herself.

''Well, do you think you could take
leadin' lady in the entertainment?''

" ' Have you ever acted any?' he asked."

Lovey Mary had no idea what the lady was expected to lead, but she knew that she was being honored, and she was thrilled at the prospect.

"I know some arm-exercises, and I could sing for them," she offered.

"Oh, no," explained Jake; "it 's a play, a reg'lar theayter play. I got the book and the costumes down on Market street. The man did n't have but this one set of costumes on hand, so I did n't have no choice. It 's a bully play, all right, though! I seen it oncet, an' I know how it all ought to go. It 's named 'Forst,' er somethin' like that. I 'm goin' to be the devil, an' wear a red suit, an' have my face all streaked up. Billy he 's goin' to be the other feller what 's stuck on the girl. He tolc me to ast you to be her. Your dress is white with cords an' tassels on it, an' the sleeves ain't sewed up. Reckon you

145

could learn the part? We ain't goin' to give it all.''

"I can learn anything!" cried Lovey Mary, recklessly. "Already know the alphabet and the Lord's Prayer backward. Is the dress short-sleeve? And does it drag in the back when you walk?"

"Yep," said Jake, "an' the man said you was to plait your hair in two parts an' let 'em hang over your shoulders. I don't see why it would n't be pretty for you to sing somethin', too. Ever'-body is so stuck on yer singin'.''

"All right," said Lovey Mary, enthusiastically; "you bring the book over and show me where my part 's at. And, Jake," she called as he started off, "you tell Billy I 'll be glad to."

For the next ten days Lovey Mary dwelt in Elysium. The prompt-book, the rehearsals, the consultations, filled the spare moments and threw a glamour over the busy ones. Jake, with his vast experience and unlimited knowledge of stage-craft, appealed to her in everything. He sat on a barrel and told how they did things "up to the opery-house," and Lovey Mary, seizing his suggestions with burning zeal, refitted the costumes, constructed scenery, hammered her own nails as well as the iron ones, and finally succeeded in putting into practice his rather vague theories. For the first time in her life she was a person of importance.

Besides her numerous other duties she prepared an elaborate costume for Tommy. This had caused her some trouble, for Miss Hazy, who was sent to buy the goods for the trousers, exercised unwise economy in buying two remnants which did not match in color or pattern.

147

"Why did n't you put your mind on it, Miss Hazy?" asked Lovey Mary, making a heroic effort to keep her temper. "You might have known I could n't take Tommy to the show with one blue leg and one brown one. What must I do?"

Miss Hazy sat dejectedly in the corner, wiping her eyes on her apron. "You might go ast Mis' Wiggs," she suggested as a forlorn hope.

When Mrs. Wiggs was told the trouble she smiled reassuringly. Emergencies were to her the spice of life; they furnished opportunities for the expression of her genius.

"Hush cryin', Miss Hazy; there ain't a speck of harm did. Mary kin make the front outen one piece an' the back outen the other. Nobody won't never know the difference, 'cause Tommy can't be goin' an' comin' at the same time."

148

The result was highly satisfactory, that is, to everybody but Tommy. He complained that there "was n't no room to set down."

On Christmas night the aristocracy of the Cabbage Patch assembled in the school-house to enjoy the double attraction of a Christmas tree and an entertainment. Mr. Rothchild, who had arranged the tree for the last ten years, refused to have it moved from its accustomed place, which was almost in the center of the platform. He had been earnestly remonstrated with, but he and the tree remained firm. Mrs. Rothchild and all the little Rothchildren had climbed in by the window before the doors were open in order to secure the front seats. Immediately behind them sat the Hazys and the Wiggses.

"That there is the seminary student gittin' up now," whispered Mrs. Wiggs.

"He 's goin' to call out the pieces. My land! ain't he washed out? Looks like he 'd go into a trance fer fifty cents. Hush, Australia! don't you see he is goin' to pray?"

After the opening prayer, the young preacher suggested that, as long as the speakers were not quite ready, the audience should "raise a hymn."

"He 's got a fine voice," whispered Miss Hazy; "I heared 'em say he was the gentleman soprano at a down-town church."

When the religious exercises were completed, the audience settled into a state of pleasurable anticipation.

"The first feature of the entertainment," announced the preacher, "will be a song by Miss Europena Wiggs."

Europena stepped forward and, with hands close to her sides and anguished

"Europena stepped forward."

eyes on the ceiling, gasped forth the agonized query:

> "Can she make a cheery-pie,
> Billy boy, Billy boy?
> Can she make a cheery-pie,
> Charming Billy?"

Notwithstanding the fact that there were eight verses, an encore was demanded. Mrs. Wiggs rose in her seat and beckoned vehemently to Europena. "Come on back!" she motioned violently with her lips. "They want you to come back."

Europena, in a state of utter bewilderment, returned to the stage.

"Say another speech!" whispered Mrs. Wiggs, leaning over so far that she knocked Mrs. Rothchild's bonnet awry. Still Europena stood there, an evident victim of lockjaw.

"'I have a little finger,'" prompted her mother frantically from the second row front.

153

A single ray of intelligence flickered for a moment over the child's face, and with a supreme effort she said:

> "I have a little finger,
>   An' I have a little beau;
> When I get a little bigger
>   I 'll have a little toe."

"'Well, she got it all in,'" said Mrs. Wiggs, in a relieved tone, as Europena was lifted down.

After this, other little girls came forward and made some unintelligible remarks concerning Santa Claus. It was with some difficulty that they went through their parts, for Mr. Rothchild kept getting in the way as he calmly and uncompromisingly continued to hang cornucopias on the tree. Songs and recitations followed, but even the youngest spectator realized that these were only preliminary skirmishes.

At last a bell rang. Two bedspreads

which served as curtains were majestically withdrawn. A sigh of admiration swept the room. "Ain't he cute!" whispered a girl in the rear, as Billy rose resplendent in pink tights and crimson doublet, and folding his arms high on his breast, recited in a deep voice:

> "I have, alas! philosophy,
>   Medicine, jurisprudence too,
>   And, to my cost, theology
>   With ardent labor studied through."

"I don't see no sense in what he 's sayin' at all," whispered Miss Hazy.

"It 's jes what was in the book," answered Mrs. Wiggs, "'cause I heared him repeat it off before supper."

The entrance of Jake awakened the flagging interest. Nobody understood what he said either, but he made horrible faces, and waved his red arms, and caused a pleasant diversion.

"Maw, what's John Bagby a-handin' round in that little saucer?" asked Australia.

"Fer the mercy sake! I don't know," answered her mother, craning her neck to see.

John, with creaking footsteps, tiptoed to the front of the stage, and stooping down, began to mix a concoction in a plate. Many stood up to see what he was doing, and conjecture was rife. *Mephisto* and *Faust* were forgotten until Jake struck a heroic pose, and grasping Billy's arm, said hoarsely:

"Gaze, Faustis, gaze into pairdition!"

John put a match to the powder, a bright red light filled the room, and the audience, following the index-finger of the impassioned *Mephisto,* gazed into the placid, stupid faces of four meek little boys on the mourners' bench.

Before the violent coughing caused

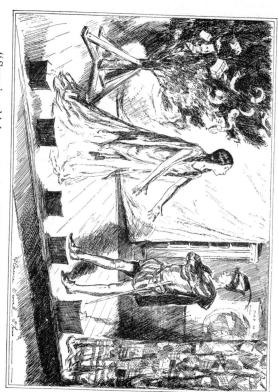

"Sang in a high, sweet voice, 'I Need Thee Every Hour.'"

by the calcium fumes had ceased, a vision in white squeezed past Mr. Rothchild and came slowly down to the edge of the platform. It was Lovey Mary as *Marguerite*. Her long dress swept about her feet, her heavy hair hung in thick braids over both shoulders, and a burning red spot glowed on each cheek. For a moment she stood as Jake had directed, with head thrown back and eyes cast heavenward, then she began to recite. The words poured from her lips with a volubility that would have shamed an auctioneer. It was a long part, full of hard words, but she knew it perfectly and was determined to show how fast she could say it without making a mistake. It was only when she finished that she paused for breath. Then she turned slowly, and stretching forth appealing arms to *Faust*, sang in a high, sweet voice, "I Need Thee Every Hour."

159

The effect was electrical. At last the Cabbage Patch understood what was going on. The roof rang with applause. Even Mr. Rothchild held aside his strings of pop-corn to let *Marguerite* pass out.

"S' more! S' more!" was the cry. "Sing it ag'in!"

Jake stepped before the curtain. "If our friends is willin'," he said, "we 'll repeat over the last ak."

Again Lovey Mary scored a triumph. John Bagby burned the rest of the calcium powder during the last verse, and the entertainment concluded in a prolonged cheer.

CHAPTER XII

REACTION

"Our remedies oft in ourselves do lie."

HEN the paint and powder had been washed off, and Tommy had with difficulty been extracted from his new trousers and put to bed, Lovey Mary sat before the little stove and thought it all over. It had been the very happiest time of her whole life. How nice it was to be praised and made much of! Mrs. Wiggs had started it by calling everybody's attention to her good points; then Mrs. Redding had sought her out and shown her continued attention; to-night was the great climax. Her name had been on every tongue, her praises sung on every side, and Billy Wiggs had given

her everything he got off the Christmas tree.

"I wisht I deserved it all," she said, as she got up to pull the blanket closer about Tommy. "I 've tried to be good. I guess I am better in some ways, but not in all—not in all." She knelt by the bed and held Tommy's hand to her cheek. "Sometimes he looks like Kate when he 's asleep like this. I wonder if she 's got well? I wonder if she ever misses him?"

For a long time she knelt there, holding the warm little hand in hers. The play, the success, the applause, were all forgotten, and in their place was a shame, a humiliation, that brought the hot tears to her eyes.

"I ain't what they think I am," she whispered brokenly. "I 'm a mean, bad girl after all. The canker-worm 's there. Miss Viny said there never would be a sure-'nough beautiful flower till the canker-worm was killed. But I want to be good; I want to be what they think I am!''

Again and again the old thoughts of Kate rose to taunt and madden her. But a new power was at work; it brought new thoughts of Kate, of Kate sick and helpless, of Kate without friends and lonely, calling for her baby. Through the night the battle raged within her. When the first gray streaks showed through the shutters, Lovey Mary cleaned her room and put on her Sunday dress. ''I 'll be a little late to the factory,'' she explained to Miss Hazy at breakfast, ''for I 've got to go on a' errand.''

It was an early hour for visitors at the city hospital, but when Lovey Mary stated her business she was shown to Kate's ward. At the far end of the

163

long room, with her bandaged head
turned to the wall, lay Kate. When the
nurse spoke to her she turned her head
painfully, and looked at them listlessly
with great black eyes that stared forth
from a face wasted and wan from suf-
fering.

"Kate!" said Lovey Mary, leaning
across the bed and touching her hand.
"Kate, don't you know me?"

The pale lips tightened over the
prominent white teeth. "Well, I swan,
Lovey Mary, where'd you come from?"
Not waiting for an answer, she continued
querulously: "Say, can't you get me
out of this hole someway? But even if
I had the strength to crawl, I wouldn't
have no place to go. Can't you take me
away? Anywhere would do."

Lovey Mary's spirits fell; she had
nerved herself for a great sacrifice, had
decided to do her duty at any cost; but

164

thinking of it beforehand in her little garret room, with Tommy's hand in hers, and Kate Rider a mere abstraction, was very different from facing the real issue, with the old, selfish, heartless Kate in flesh and blood before her. She let go of Kate's hand.

"Don't you want to know about Tommy?" she asked. "I 've come to say I was sorry I run off with him."

"It was mighty nervy in you. I knew you 'd take good care of him, though. But say! you can get me away from this, can't you? I ain't got a friend in the world nor a cent of money. But I ain't going to stay here, where there ain't nothing to do, and I get so lonesome I 'most die. I 'd rather set on a street corner and run a hand-organ. Where are you and Tommy at?"

"We are in the Cabbage Patch," said

Lovey Mary, with the old repulsion strong upon her.

"Where?"

"The Cabbage Patch. It ain't your sort of a place, Kate. The folks are good and honest, but they are poor and plain. You 'd laugh at 'em."

Kate turned her eyes to the window and was silent a moment before she said slowly:

"I ain't got much right to laugh at nobody. I 'd be sorter glad to get with good people again. The other sort 's all right when you 're out for fun, but when you 're down on your luck they ain't there."

Lovey Mary, perplexed and troubled, looked at her gravely.

"Have n't you got any place you could go to?"

Kate shook her head. "Nobody would be willing to look after me and nurse

166

"'Have n't you got any place you could go to?'"

me. Lovey,"—she stretched her thin hand across to her entreatingly,—"take me home with you! I heard the doctor tell the nurse he could n't do nothing more for me. I can't die here shut up with all these sick people. Take me wherever you are at. I 'll try not to be no trouble, and—I want to keep straight."

Tears were in her eyes, and her lips trembled. There was a queer little spasm at Lovey Mary's heart. The canker-worm was dead.

When a carriage drove up to Miss Hazy's door and the driver carried in a pale girl with a bandaged head, it caused untold commotion.

"Do you s'pose Mary 's a-bringin' home a smallpox patient?" asked Miss Hazy, who was ever prone to look upon the tragic side.

"Naw!" said Chris, who was peeping under the window-curtain; "it looks more like she 's busted her crust."

In less than an hour every neighbor had been in to find out what was going on. Mrs. Wiggs constituted herself mistress of ceremonies. She had heard the whole story from the overburdened Mary, and was now prepared to direct public opinion in the way it should go.

"Jes another boarder for Miss Hazy," she explained airily to Mrs. Eichorn. "Lovey Mary was so well pleased with her boardin'-house, she drummed it up among her friends. This here lady has been at the hospittal. She got knocked over by a wagon out there near the factory, an' it run into celebrated concussion. The nurse told Lovey Mary this mornin' it was somethin' like information of the brain. What we 're all goin' to do is to try to get her well. I 'm a-goin' home now to git her a nice dinner, an' I jes bet some of you 'll see to it that she gits a good supper. You kin jes bank on us knowin' how to give a stranger a welcome!''

It was easy to establish a precedent in the Cabbage Patch. When a certain course of action was once understood to be the proper thing, every resident promptly fell in line. The victim of ''celebrated concussion'' was overwhelmed with attention. She lay in a pink wrapper in Miss Hazy's kitchen, and received the homage of the neighborhood. Meanwhile Lovey Mary worked extra hours at the factory and did sewing at night to pay for Kate's board.

In spite, however, of the kind treatment and the regular administration of Miss Viny's herbs and Mrs. Wiggs's yellowroot, Kate grew weaker day by day. One stormy night when Lovey Mary came home from the factory she found her burning with fever and talking excitedly. Miss Hazy had gotten her up-stairs, and now stood helplessly wringing her hands in the doorway.

"Lor', Lovey Mary! she 's cuttin' up scandalous," complained the old lady. "I done ever'thing I knowed how; I ironed the sheets to make 'em warm, an' I tried my best to git her to swallow a mustard cocktail. I wanted her to lemme put a fly-blister on to her head, too, but she won't do nothin'."

"All right, Miss Hazy," said Lovey Mary, hanging her dripping coat on a nail. "I 'll stay with her now. Don't talk, Kate! Try to be still."

"But I can't, Lovey. I 'm going to die, and I ain't fit to die. I 've been so bad and wicked, I 'm 'fraid to go, Lovey. What 'll I do? What 'll I do?"

172

In vain the girl tried to soothe her. Her hysteria increased; she cried and raved and threw herself from side to side.

"Kate! Kate!" pleaded Lovey Mary, trying to hold her arms, "don't cry so. God 'll forgive you. He will, if you are sorry."

"But I 'm afraid," shuddered Kate. "I 've been so bad. Heaven knows I 'm sorry, but it 's too late! Too late!" Another paroxysm seized her, and her cries burst forth afresh.

Mary, in desperation, rushed from the room. "Tommy!" she called softly down the steps.

The small boy was sitting on the stairs, in round-eyed wonder at what was going on.

"Tommy," said Lovey Mary, picking him up, "the sick lady feels so bad! Go in and give her a love, darling. Pet

173

her cheeks and hug her like you do me. Tell her she 's a pretty mama. Tell her you love her.''

Tommy trotted obediently into the low room and climbed on the bed. He put his plump cheek against the thin one, and whispered words of baby-love. Kate's muscles relaxed as her arms folded about him. Gradually her sobs ceased and her pulse grew faint and fainter. Outside, the rain and sleet beat on the cracked window-pane, but a peace had entered the dingy little room. Kate received the great summons with a smile, for in one fleeting moment she had felt for the first and last time the blessed sanctity of motherhood.

CHAPTER XIII

AN HONORABLE RETREAT

"For I will ease my heart
 Although it be with hazard
 Of my head."

ISS BELL sat in her
neat little office, with the
evening paper in her
hand. The hour before
tea was the one time of
the day she reserved for herself. Susie
Smithers declared that she sat before
the fire at such times and took naps, but
Susie's knowledge was not always trust-
worthy—it depended entirely on the
position of the keyhole.

At any rate, Miss Bell was not sleeping to-night; she moved about restlessly,
brushing imaginary ashes from the spot-

less hearth, staring absently into the fire, then recurring again and again to an item in the paper which she held:

DIED. Kate Rider, in her twenty-fourth year, from injuries received in an accident.

Miss Bell seemed to cringe before the words. Her face looked old and drawn. "And to think I kept her from having her child!" she said to herself as she paced up and down the narrow room. "No matter what else Kate was, she was his mother and had the first right to him. But I acted for the best; I could see no other way. If I had only known!"

There were steps on the pavement without; she went to the window, and shading her eyes with her hands, gazed into the gathering dusk. Some one was coming up the walk, some one very short and fat. No; it was a girl carry-

"Susie Smithers at the keyhole."

ing a child. Miss Bell reached the door
just in time to catch Tommy in her arms
as Lovey Mary staggered into the hall.
They were covered with sleet and almost
numb from the cold.

"Kate 's dead!" cried Lovey Mary,
as Miss Bell hurried them into the office.
"I did n't know she was going to die.
Oh, I 've been so wicked to you and to
Kate and to God! I want to be arrested!
I don't care what they do to me."

She threw herself on the floor, and
beat her fists on the carpet. Tommy
stood near and wept in sympathy; he
wore his remnant trousers, and his little
straw hat, round which Mrs. Wiggs had
sewn a broad band of black.

Miss Bell hovered over Lovey Mary
and patted her nervously on the back.
"Don't, my dear, don't cry so. It 's
very sad—dear me, yes, very sad. You
are n't alone to blame, though; I have

been at fault, too. I—I—feel dread-fully about it.''

Miss Bell's face was undergoing such painful contortions that Lovey Mary stopped crying in alarm, and Tommy got behind a chair.

"Of course," continued Miss Bell, gaining control of herself, "it was very wrong of you to run away, Mary. When I discovered that you had gone I never stopped until I found you."

"Till you found me?" gasped Lovey Mary.

"Yes, child; I knew where you were all the time."

Again Miss Bell's features were convulsed, and Mary and Tommy looked on in awed silence. "You see," she went on presently, "I am just as much at fault as you. I was worried and distressed over having to let Tommy go with Kate, yet there seemed no way out

180

of it. When I found you had hidden him away in a safe place, that you were both well and happy, I determined to keep your secret. But oh, Mary, we had n't the right to keep him from her! Perhaps the child would have been her salvation; perhaps she would have died a good girl.''

''But she did, Miss Bell,'' said Lovey Mary, earnestly. ''She said she was sorry again and again, and when she went to sleep Tommy's arms was round her neck.''

''Mary!'' cried Miss Bell, seizing the girl's hand eagerly, ''did you find her and take him to her?''

''No, ma'am. I brought her to him. She did n't have no place to go, and I wanted to make up to her for hating her so. I did ever'thing I could to make her well. We all did. I never thought she was going to die.''

Then, at Miss Bell's request, Lovey Mary told her story, with many sobs and tears, but some smiles in between, over the good times in the Cabbage Patch; and when she had finished, Miss Bell led her over to the sofa and put her arms about her. They had lived under the same roof for fifteen years, and she had never before given her a caress.

"Mary," she said, "you did for Kate what nobody else could have done. I thank God that it all happened as it did."

"But you 'd orter scold me and punish me," said Lovey Mary. "I 'd feel better if you did."

Tommy, realizing in some vague way that a love-feast was in progress, and always ready to echo Lovey Mary's sentiments, laid his chubby hand on Miss Bell's knee.

"When my little sled drows up I 'm

doin' to take you ridin'," he said con-
fidingly.

Miss Bell laughed a hearty laugh, for
the first time in many months. The
knotty problem which had caused her
many sleepless nights had at last found
its own solution.

CHAPTER XIV

THE CACTUS BLOOMS

"I tell thee love is nature's second sun,
Causing a spring of virtues where he shines."

T was June again, and once more Lovey Mary stood at an up-stairs window at the home. On the ledge grew a row of bright flowers, brought from Miss Viny's garden, but they were no brighter than the face that smiled across them at the small boy in the playground below. Lovey Mary's sleeves were rolled above her elbows, and a dust-cloth was tied about her head. As she returned to her sweeping she sang joyfully, contentedly:

"Can she sweep a kitchen floor,
Billy boy, Billy boy?

184

Can she sweep a kitchen floor,
   Charming Billy?"

"Miss Bell says for you to come down to the office," announced a little girl, coming up the steps. "There 's a lady there and a baby."

Lovey Mary paused in her work, and a shadow passed over her face. Just three years ago the same summons had come, and with it such heartaches and anxiety. She pulled down her sleeves and went thoughtfully down the steps. At the office door she found Mrs. Redding talking to Miss Bell.

"We leave Saturday afternoon," she was saying. "It 's rather sooner than we expected, but we want to get the baby to Canada before the hot weather overtakes us. Last summer I asked two children from the Toronto home to spend two weeks with me at our summer place, but this year I have set my heart

185

on taking Lovey Mary and Tommy.
They will see Niagara Falls and Buffalo, where we stop over a day, besides
the little outing at the lake. Will you
come, Mary? You know Robert might
get choked again!"

Lovey Mary leaned against the door
for support. A half-hour visit to Mrs.
Redding was excitement for a week, and
only to think of going away with her,
and riding on a steam-car, and seeing a
lake, and taking Tommy, and being ever
so small a part of that gorgeous Redding household! She could not speak;
she just looked up and smiled, but the
smile seemed to mean more than words,
for it brought the sudden tears to Mrs.
Redding's eyes. She gave Mary's hand
a quick, understanding little squeeze,
then hurried out to her carriage.

That very afternoon Lovey Mary
went to the Cabbage Patch. As she hur-

ried along over the familiar ground, she felt as if she must sing aloud the happy song that was humming in her heart. She wanted to stop at each cottage and tell the good news; but her time was limited, so she kept on her way to Miss Hazy's, merely calling out a greeting as she passed. When she reached the door she heard Mrs. Wiggs's voice in animated conversation.

"Well, I wish you 'd look! There she is, this very minute! I never was so glad to see anybody in my life! My goodness, child, you don't know how we miss you down here! We talk 'bout you all the time, jes like a person puts their tongue in the empty place after a tooth 's done pulled out."

"I 'm awful glad to be back," said Lovey Mary, too happy to be cast down by the reversion to the original state of the Hazy household.

"Me an' Chris ain't had a comfortable day sence you left," complained Miss Hazy. "I 'd 'a' almost rather you would n't 'a' came than to have went away ag'in."

"But listen!" cried Lovey Mary, unable to keep her news another minute. "I 'm a-going on a railroad trip with Mrs. Redding, and she 's going to take Tommy, too, and we are going to see Niag'ra and a lake and a buffalo!"

"Ain't that the grandest thing fer her to go and do!" exclaimed Mrs. Wiggs. "I told you she was a' angel!"

"I 'm right skeered of these here long trips," said Miss Hazy, "so many accidents these days."

"My sakes!" answered Mrs. Wiggs, "I 'd think you 'd be 'fraid to step over a crack in the floor fer fear you 'd fall through. Why, Lovey Mary, it 's the nicest thing I ever heared tell of! An'

Niag'ry Fall, too. I went on a trip once
when I was little. Maw took me through
the mountains. I never had seen mountains before, an' I cried at first an'
begged her to make 'em sit down. A trip
is something you never will fergit in all
yer life. It was jes like Mrs. Reddin'
to think about it; but I don't wonder
she feels good to you. Asia says she
never expects to see anything like the
way you shook that candy outen little
Robert. But see here, if you go 'way off
there you must n't fergit us.''

''I never could forget you all, wherever I went,'' said Lovey Mary. ''I
was awful mean when I come to the
Cabbage Patch; somehow you all just
bluffed me into being better. I was n't
used to being bragged on, and it made
me want to be good more than anything
in the world.''

''That 's so,'' said Mrs. Wiggs. ''You

can coax a' elephant with a little sugar.
The worser Mr. Wiggs used to act, the
harder I 'd pat him on the back. When
he 'd git bilin' mad, I 'd say: 'Now, Mr.
Wiggs, why don't you go right out in
the woodshed an' swear off that cuss?
I hate to think of it rampantin' round
inside of a good-lookin' man like you.'
He 'd often take my advice, an' it always done him good an' never hurt the
woodshed. As fer the childern, I always
did use compelments on them 'stid of
switches.''

Lovey Mary untied the bundle which
she carried, and spread the contents on
the kitchen table. ''I 've been saving
up to get you all some presents,'' she
said. ''I wanted to get something for
every one that had been good to me, but
that took in the whole Patch! These
are some new kind of seed for Miss
Viny; she learned me a lot out of her

garden. This is goods for a waist for you, Miss Hazy.''

''It 's rale pretty,'' said Miss Hazy, measuring its length. ''If you 'd 'a' brought me enough fer a skirt, too, I 'd never 'a' got through prayin' fer you.''

Mrs. Wiggs was indignant. ''I declare, Miss Hazy! You ain't got a manner in the world, sometimes. It 's beautiful goods, Lovey Mary. I 'm goin' to make it up fer her by a fancy new pattern Asia bought; it 's got a sailor collar.''

''This here is for Chris,'' continued Lovey Mary, slightly depressed by Miss Hazy's lack of appreciation, ''and this is for Mrs. Schultz. I bought you a book, Mrs. Wiggs. I don't know what it 's about, but it 's an awful pretty cover. I knew you 'd like to have it on the parlor table.''

It was the ''Iliad''!

Mrs. Wiggs held it at arm's-length and, squinting her eyes, read: "Home of an Island."

"That ain't what the man called it," said Lovey Mary.

"Oh, it don't matter 'bout the name. It 's a beautiful book, jes matches my new tidy. You could n't 'a' pleased me better."

"I did n't have money enough to go round," explained Lovey Mary, apologetically, "but I bought a dozen lead-pencils and thought I 'd give them round among the children."

"Ever'thing 'll be terrible wrote over," said Miss Hazy.

The last bundle was done up in tissue-paper and tied with a silver string. Lovey Mary gave it to Mrs. Wiggs when Miss Hazy was not looking.

"It 's a red necktie," she whispered, "for Billy."

When the train for the North pulled out of the station one Saturday afternoon it bore an excited passenger. Lovey Mary, in a new dress and hat, sat on the edge of a seat, with little Robert on one side and Tommy on the other. When her nervousness grew unbearable she leaned forward and touched Mrs. Redding on the shoulder:

"Will you please, ma'am, tell me when we get there?"

Mrs. Redding laughed. "Get there, dear? Why, we have just started!"

"I mean to the Cabbage Patch. They're all going to be watching for me as we go through."

"Is that it?" said Mr. Redding. "Well, I will take the boys, and you can go out and stand on the platform and watch for your friends."

Lovey Mary hesitated. "Please, sir, can't I take Tommy, too? If it had n't

193

'a' been for him I never would have been here.''

So Mr. Redding took them to the rear car, and attaching Lovey Mary firmly to the railing, and Tommy firmly to Mary, returned to his family.

''There 's Miss Viny's!'' cried Lovey Mary, excitedly, as the train whizzed past. ''We 're getting there. Hold on to your hat, Tommy, and get your pocket-handkerchief ready to wave.''

The bell began to ring, and the train slowed up at the great water-tank.

''There they are! All of 'em. Hello, Miss Hazy! And there 's Asia and Chris and ever'body!''

Mrs. Wiggs pushed through the little group and held an empty bottle toward Lovey Mary. ''I want you to fill it fer me,'' she cried breathlessly. ''Fill it full of Niag'ry water. I want to see how them falls look.''